MW00424523

JESSICA BECK

THE DONUT MYSTERIES, BOOK 29

TASTY TRIALS

Donut Mystery #29 Tasty Trials
Copyright © 2017 by Jessica Beck All rights reserved.
First Edition: February 2017

No part of this book may be reproduced, scanned, or distributed in any printed or electronic form without permission. Please do not participate in or encourage piracy of copyrighted materials in violation of the author's rights. This is a work of fiction. Names, characters, places, and incidents either are the product of the author's imagination or are used fictitiously, and any resemblance to actual persons, living or dead, business establishments, events, or locales is entirely coincidental.

Recipes included in this book are to be recreated at the reader's own risk. The author is not responsible for any damage, medical or otherwise, created as a result of reproducing these recipes. It is the responsibility of the reader to ensure that none of the ingredients are detrimental to their health, and the author will not be held liable in any way for any problems that might arise from following the included recipes.

The First Time Ever Published!

The 29th Donut Mystery.

Jessica Beck is the *New York Times* Bestselling Author of the
Donut Mysteries, the Classic Diner Mysteries, the Ghost
Cat Cozy Mysteries, and the Cast Iron Cooking Mysteries.

For absent friends, one of my favorite toasts in the world!

When Suzanne and Jake win a weekend getaway to a luxury resort island in the mountains, they think they're in for the time of their lives. Little do they know that they've actually been brought there to help uncover who tried to kill their host. As the married team dig deeper into the case, they are soon isolated on the island with not only more potential victims but the would-be killer as well.

CHAPTER 1

WHY IS IT THAT SOME things that seem so wonderful at first blush turn into disasters so soon after? I'm not talking about love at the moment, though there are plenty of cases where that description qualifies beautifully, but in *all* manner of things. For example, I never dreamed that winning something so fabulous could lead me into a situation where lives were put at risk by a killer, but that was how it all started that fateful day in the dregs of winter when I first got the message that we had won a contest we'd never entered.

"Are you Suzanne Hart?" the delivery woman asked me as she walked into my donut shop and headed straight toward the counter I was currently cleaning. She was in her midtwenties, and despite the cold weather, she was dressed in the firm's unflattering shorts and top. I was certain that she must be freezing, but if she was, she didn't show it. I didn't recognize her. Then again, contrary to popular belief, I didn't know *everyone* who stepped foot inside Donut Hearts, or even lived in April Springs, the part of North Carolina my husband, Jake, and I called home. The young woman was holding a large envelope in one hand, and she frowned as she looked at me. "If you're Mrs. Hart, I need you to sign for this before I can give it to you."

"Actually, it's Ms.," I corrected her automatically. I'd been a Hart all of my life until I took my first husband's last name when we'd wed, but I'd dropped it instantly upon our acrimonious divorce, and I'd vowed never to change it again. That was all well before I'd met Jake, though. My legal name was now Mrs. Suzanne Hart Bishop, but everyone usually just called me Suzanne. Since my shop was named after me, Heart substituting for Hart, I'd decided that it would just be easier to keep being known as Suzanne Hart on everything but our joint checking account and any official document I might need to sign, and my husband was fine with that. He had my heart, and he knew it. It was plenty enough for him, and me as well.

The delivery woman didn't need to know all of that, though. "Sally" was embroidered on her shirt, and I wondered how many of them just like it she had hanging in her closet at home. I smiled at her as I finally admitted, "I'm Suzanne Hart."

Sally seemed bored with the entire process as she gave me her small handheld device before parting with the envelope in question. "Cool. Just sign here, and it's yours."

As I scrawled out an illegible curvy line that looked nothing like my actual signature on the small electronic screen, Sally looked around Donut Hearts. "Is selling donuts *all* that you do here?"

"No. Not only do we sell a few other treats as well, we offer coffee and hot chocolate, too," I said, suddenly feeling the need to defend my business, as well as my way of life, to this young stranger. "Not everything's sugary, either. There are a few choices for someone who doesn't even have a sweet tooth." My best friend Grace had once been on an extended health kick where she wouldn't eat *any* of my pastry treats, but her rigorous diet had eased quite a bit over the past few years. To my constant bewilderment, somehow she hadn't gained any weight from the increased caloric intake, staying as trim and fit as she'd been in high school. I, on the other hand, had added at least twenty pounds since we'd graduated, but my mother liked to say that it had just rounded me out, whatever that was supposed to mean.

"Got it," was all she said as she took her handheld computer back and handed me the envelope before scooting out of my shop.

As the door opened, I took in a deep breath of the fresh outside air, forgetting the envelope for the moment. I loved this time of year, with the constant chill and the ever-hopeful promise of snow all around, which was rarely, if ever, fulfilled in April Springs. At least it was cold enough for the woodstoves around town that generated cozy aromas and produced lazy plumes of white smoke as long-dead leaves skittered across the pavement in the slightest whisper of wind. Emma and I had gotten into the spirit of the season just after Christmas, offering snowman-shaped donuts iced in glittering white. We'd even decorated the front window of the donut shop with canned spray snow and colorful twinkling lights, despite the fact that the holiday season had come and gone nearly two months earlier.

"What's in the package?" George Morris, our mayor and a very dear friend of mine, asked me as I studied the label after Sally left. He'd been sitting at the bar nursing a hot chocolate for most of the morning, and I could tell that whatever was waiting for him at City Hall was not all that welcome.

"I'm not sure," I said as I tried to make out the name in the upper left corner of the packet.

"Well, open it up and find out, woman," he said impatiently.

I laughed a bit before I answered. "What's the rush?" I asked him as I put the envelope down on the counter behind me. "What are you doing loitering around my shop for most of the morning, anyway?" I asked with a grin. "Don't you have any official town duties you should be seeing to?"

"Of course I do. Why do you think I've been loitering here all day?" he asked. George looked at his watch. "I've pushed things as far as I can, though. I've got a meeting in ten minutes with Van Rayburn, and frankly, I don't want to go. I once saw a sign in someone's office that said, *I don't want to, and you can't make me.* I wish I had one of those right about now."

"I completely understand the sentiment, but we both know that it's not going to help matters if you're late. I've had a few brushes with Mr. Rayburn in the past myself, so I get it. Besides, not that I don't enjoy your company, but it's nearly closing time, so if you stick around here too much longer, you're going to have to help Emma and me clean up."

"Believe me, that would be preferable to taking this meeting." George started for the door, and then he hesitated. "You're really *not* going to open that right away, are you? Suzanne, it could be important."

"I doubt it, but whatever it is, it's going to have to wait until I'm finished here for the day."

"I've got to say, you have more self-restraint than I do," George answered.

"I sincerely hope not," I said. "Good luck with your meeting."

"Thanks, but no amount of luck is going to help me get through it."

"That's what you get for being the mayor around here," I told him.

"I suppose so. Sometimes I wish I'd never quit being a cop. It was a lot easier on my nerves back then, and there are times when it even seems less dangerous. If there's anything in there you need to talk about, give me a call, okay? I'm here for you."

What an odd thing to say. "I appreciate that. Have a good meeting."

"Doubtful, but thanks for the sentiment." The mayor waved absently at me as he went out the door, and I glanced at the clock on the wall. We were two minutes away from our official closing time, and I glanced back at the envelope, wondering what might be inside. Maybe I'd just take a quick peek to see what someone had sent me. What could it hurt? It wasn't every day I got something hand-delivered to Donut Hearts from a courier service, and I was starting to get curious about its contents.

I was just reaching for it when Emma came out from the kitchen. She was my young assistant at Donut Hearts, but she was so much more than that to me, almost like the daughter I'd never had, though I was still young enough to have one of my own if I wanted. That was the one thing Jake and I never talked about. He'd lost his first wife in a car accident years before, and she'd been pregnant with their only child. The tragedy had nearly destroyed him, and though I wanted a family of my own someday, I wasn't about to be the one who brought it up.

At least not yet.

"I thought I heard something going on out here. What did we get in the mail?" Emma asked the moment she spotted the envelope on the counter.

"*We* didn't get anything," I said with a smile. "It's addressed to me personally, not the shop."

"Okay, I'll bite. What did *you* get?"

"I don't know. I'll open it later," I said, deciding to put it off until I could devote more attention to it. "What do you say we close the shop early?"

Emma glanced at the clock and grinned at me. "Wow. A full two minutes ahead of schedule? Are you sure?"

"Why not? Let's live life on the edge," I answered, matching her smile with one of my own.

"That sounds great to me. The dishes are done, so I can take these trays and cups back and knock them out in no time. What do you want to do with the leftover donuts today?"

"Do you want them?" I asked. I usually donated our extras to the church, but I had a feeling they weren't being greeted as enthusiastically as they had once been, due to our surplus of unsold goodies lately. It was a constant battle matching our offerings with the demand, but I hated running out of product a great deal more than I did having any treats left over at the end of the day.

"Sure. I'll take them to class with me. Everybody *loves* me when I bring your goodies, including the professor."

"It's settled, then. Now let's get cracking and knock this out so you can be on your way. I don't want you to be late for class."

Emma and I went through our regular routine as soon as I locked the front door and flipped the sign. The cash register report balanced out, and I had the deposit made up in record time. As I finished sweeping the front after wiping the tables down and putting the chairs upside down on them, Emma came out and whistled. "Wow, you were really on fire today. Is there somewhere you need to be that I don't know about?"

"Nothing in particular. I'm just eager to see my husband," I said with a smile.

"If that's the case, then you're not going to have to wait long," my assistant said as she pointed to the front door, grinning.

Sure enough, Jake Bishop was standing just outside, smiling warmly at me. He was a retired investigator for the state police, and I was getting the sense that he was growing bored with his recent inactivity. I'd been wracking my brain trying to come up with something for him to do, and I'd even offered him a spare office I'd inherited from my late father to use as a private detective agency, but so far, Jake had shown little inclination of doing it. Still, there had to be *something* he could do to fill his time while I was running my donut shop. We just hadn't come up with any ideas yet. I couldn't even say that he might *not* eventually start his own PI business sometime in the future. Only time would tell. Where my husband was concerned, life traveled at its own pace, and woe to the person who tried to rush him into anything he wasn't ready for.

I unlocked the front door, and before Jake could get inside, Emma slipped out, her arms laden with boxes of donuts. "Hey, Jake. Bye, Jake. See you in a few days, Suzanne."

"Bye. Now don't forget, you can always call me if you need me," I said. It was Emma and her mother's turn to take over the shop for the next two days, a policy I'd instituted so I could spend more time with my husband.

"You know I won't, but it's nice knowing you're just a few steps away in case I do."

"I'll be ready in one second," I told Jake after giving him a quick kiss. "How's your morning been so far?"

"The same as the one before it, and the one before that," he said with a soft smile.

"You're not getting bored with me already, are you?"

My husband took me in his arms, and I marveled yet again at just how good it felt. "You? Never. My situation? Maybe. Suzanne, I've been thinking. I'm not exactly sure that I'm cut out for retirement quite yet. In some ways, I'm still a relatively young man."

"I've been thinking the same thing myself," I said. "Have you been able to come up with anything?"

"Not yet, but I'm working on it," he said with a somber expression. "Give me a little time to ponder. I'm sure that it'll come to me. Are you ready?"

"Let's go," I said as I glanced around the shop one last time. That was when I spied the envelope on the counter. "Hang on. I nearly forgot something."

"What's that?"

"I have no idea," I admitted as I handed him my deposit bag for the bank. "Let's open it up and see, shall we?"

Before we headed outside, I tore into the envelope.

The document inside had been printed in an ornate font on expensive paper that made it appear to be two hundred years old, though it was clear that wasn't the case. It said:

"To Suzanne Hart and Jake Bishop,

Congratulations. Your names were submitted by guests at our retreat earlier this year, and you've been chosen to enjoy three nights and four days at the Star Island Retreat, with our compliments. All expenses will be paid, and while you will be our guests, your every whim* will be accommodated. To redeem this prize, please contact the telephone number printed below by twelve noon, February Nineteenth**. We look forward to hearing from you soon.

Sincerely,

The management and staff of Star Island Retreat***"

"Suzanne, that's today," Jake said as he frowned at the letter I'd just received. After glancing at his watch, he said, "Not only that, but you've got exactly thirty-seven minutes to redeem it. That's cutting it pretty close, isn't it?"

I nodded. "What I'm wondering is why it took three sets of asterisks for one short letter," I said as I read aloud what was printed below the first asterisk, which had come after the word "whim." I told my husband, "Jake, according to this, our whim redemptions are *at the sole discretion of management.*" As I kept reading, I shared the rest of the explanations, emphasizing the words used as clarifications. "The double asterisk says, '*The trip must begin on February Nineteenth of the current year. No substitutions of winners or dates are allowed, and if attempted, it will result in the complete and instant revocation of this prize.*'"

"So, it's ours, and only ours," Jake said. "If we choose not to use it, no one else can either."

"That's only fair, don't you think?" I asked. It sounded like an adventure to me, and my husband and I both needed something to shake up our routines. It wasn't that we were getting bored with each other, but this sounded like an opportunity that was too good to pass up.

There was a triple asterisk keyed to the end of the last "Retreat," and I read it aloud in its entirety. "*We are not responsible for any and all events that may transpire at the retreat during your stay. All taxes owed by the winners will be paid by the owners of the Star Island Retreat. Your signature on a full waiver will be required upon check-in, and the retreat will not be liable for anything that may happen during your stay."*

"I don't know," Jake said. "It sounds fishy to me. Have you ever heard of this Star Island Retreat?"

"Vaguely. It's somewhere in the mountains above Asheville, I believe," I said as I took out my cell phone and checked it out through a search engine. After looking up the resort's name and reading a few entries, I said, "It looks legit to me. Evidently the place is owned and operated by somebody named H. J. Castor. It's on an island in the middle of a mountain lake, and it got its name from the star shape of the land. Wow, look at these rates," I said as I showed Jake a screenshot of their prices.

After whistling softly to himself, my husband said, "We couldn't afford this on our own. What do you think? Should we do it?"

"Why not? I'm sure Emma and Sharon will cover the shop for an extra day. How frequently do we get a trip like this that lands in our laps, with no strings attached?"

"Not very often at all," Jake said a little too quietly for my taste.

"I wonder who nominated us? We really should thank them," I said happily. "Maybe a nice bottle of wine, or even a dozen donuts."

"Yes, I suppose," Jake said, clearly distracted by something.

"Aren't you excited?"

"If it's real, yes, of course I am," he said reluctantly.

"Why are you being so cynical about this?" I asked as I dialed the number provided to confirm our visit. "Trust me. I'm sure everything will be absolutely lovely." I've said more than my share of boneheaded things in the past, but that may have topped the list, when all was said and done. Soon enough, things would be far from fine indeed, and I quickly found myself regretting ever responding to the offer that turned out to be, as my husband had suspected, too good to be true, after all.

CHAPTER 2

"**I**s that the dock up ahead?" I asked Jake as I drove down the snowy lane toward the lake. We'd been on the road nearly two hours, and I knew that we had to be getting close. Emma had been more than happy to work an extra day, so Jake and I had made the call reserving our place at the retreat—despite his initial reluctance—packed our bags, and we were on our way. We'd decided to take my Jeep since there was a forecast of snow in the mountains, and Jake's truck was next to worthless in the potentially slippery conditions we might face. I was glad we'd chosen to do that as we kept heading down the lane. The snow flurries had started just south of Asheville, and by the time we'd driven another twenty miles north into the mountains, the snow had begun to fall in earnest.

"I sure hope so, but I can't see much in this mess," Jake answered as he kept glancing up at the white sky. "It's really starting to come down, isn't it?"

"I know. It's exciting, isn't it?"

"Suzanne, you can think of this as some kind of winter-wonderland adventure if you want to, but I need to go on record that I'm reserving judgment until we see just how bad this weather is going to get," he said as he glanced skyward again. "What's a big snowfall going to do to the services on the island? Do we have to worry about losing power? How about heat? Hopefully we'll be able to get back to April Springs when this is all over."

I frowned at my husband for a moment, and then I poked him and smiled as I said, "Come on, don't be that way! You need to lighten up and get into the spirit of this with me, okay? Let's think of it as an adventure we'd never be able to afford on our own."

My husband paused for a moment, and then he offered me a slight smile. "You're right. I'm sorry. I'll do my best."

"Good," I said as I patted his knee. "Now, I have an important question for you."

"I'll answer it if I can," he said solemnly.

I grinned as I asked him, "You said that you were worried that we might lose our heat if the storm gets too bad. Will that really matter if we have a fireplace in our room? You *do* think we'll have one, don't you?"

Jake lightened considerably at the sound of playfulness in my voice. "I'm willing to bet there's going to be *at least* one in every room," he said with a grin. Maybe my good mood was infectious, or perhaps he was just trying to convince us both that he was going to enjoy our time at the resort. Either way, it meant a lot to me that he was trying. I planned on having a good time, and what was more, I was determined to make sure that my husband did as well.

As we got closer to the end of the road and took the final bend, I saw that there was a small covered dock on the water, so I parked in a lot to one side that was already in heavy use. There were half a dozen cars already there, a mix of luxury cars and a few vehicles that appeared to be barely held together with duct tape and baling wire. Jake and I each grabbed the small bags we'd packed for our trip, I locked the Jeep, and we hurried to the shelter. I was relieved when we got there to see that someone was waiting for us, and as we approached the figure, I took in the tall, shapely young woman, more cute than pretty, and most likely somewhere around Emma's age. She had long, curly black hair that cascaded down her shoulders and the darkest eyes I'd ever seen in my life, but her smile was enough to brighten even the most dimly lit corner of any space.

"You must be Mr. and Mrs. Bishop," she said as she offered to take our bags. "I'm Cyn," she said, offering us a crooked little smile.

"Pardon me?" Jake asked. "Did you just say your name was Sin?"

"Yes, but it's spelled C-Y-N," she said as she spelled out the letters, "not the S-I-N you're probably thinking. What can I say? I'm a good girl with a bad name." Cyn grinned automatically at her joke, no doubt one she often told strangers upon first meeting. Against Jake's protests, Cyn took our bags, but instead of stowing them in the small boat tied up nearby, she put them on the covered bench beside us.

"It's good to meet you, Cyn," I said with a genuine smile as I offered her my hand. "I'm Suzanne, and this is Jake. We're not too crazy about being addressed as Mr. and Mrs. Bishop."

"Got it," the young woman said, matching my grin with a powerful one of her own. That smile was quite a bit more genuine than the one she'd given us out of habit after telling us about her name. "You each read the fine print in your letter, right?"

"Which part?" I asked. "I'll be honest with you. I was really sad when I saw that my whims were going to be so narrowly interpreted."

"Yeah, that part was a hoot, wasn't it? I'm talking about the waiver the letter mentioned. Do you have any objections to signing it? The reason I ask is that a few folks have been reluctant to agree to Hodge's terms. It's entirely up to you."

"I'd like to read the document myself before I answer that, if you wouldn't mind," Jake said.

"Of course," Cyn said as she walked over to a covered box and pulled out two copies, already attached to clipboards. After she handed them to us, she retreated to a portable heater and promptly ignored us as she watched the snow vanish as it fell into the lake.

As I read the fine print of the document she'd just given us, I realized that the waiver covered the owner's liability for anything up to and including tidal waves and asteroid strikes, but I knew I was going to sign anyway. After all, the best parts of life often came with risk, and if something did happen to me on the island, I doubted my first reaction would be to sue our host. My philosophy was that if I didn't take any chances, if I tried to live my life constantly being safely ensconced in bubble wrap, could I really claim to be alive?

I took the pen and happily scrawled out my name before handing the waiver back to Cyn.

When I looked up, I found my husband frowning at me. "Suzanne, are you sure about this?"

"I don't know about you, but I'm not about to let this document ruin what is probably going to be a wonderful vacation. If you don't want to sign it, I completely understand. Feel free to take the Jeep back home. Just don't forget to come back here in four days to pick me up," I added with a grin, knowing that there was no way Jake would ever do anything of the sort.

As predicted, my husband shrugged, signed his own form, and then he handed it back to Cyn as well.

"Has anyone actually refused to sign it?" I asked her.

"Are you kidding? It's four free days at a five-star retreat for each of our guests. There were a few grumbles, but believe me, everyone ended up signing." Cyn glanced toward the water, which had begun to get a little choppy in the growing wind. The snowfall, if anything, had intensified. "Are you folks ready? I'd like to cross while I can still see the island, if it's all the same to you."

After Jake and I got into the small boat—no more than a fisherman's skiff really—Cyn expertly stowed our bags under a tarp, untied our line, started the boat's small engine with a single pull, and then headed away from the mainland toward the island ahead, now lost in the falling snow. "Now's as good a time as any to give you a little history of Star Island," Cyn said above the dull roar of the motor. At that moment, nearly as quickly as it had first begun, the snow came to an abrupt halt, petering out into nothing in the span of a single heartbeat. It was as though someone had thrown a switch cutting off the supply from above, and it had done its job in an instant.

"It's absolutely crazy that the snow just stopped like that," I said.

"Actually, it's not that unusual around here," Cyn replied. "Next week, they're saying we're going to get really slammed, but no worries. You'll be out of here in plenty of time. Right now, though, you'll have some beautiful scenery on the Star. That's what we call it among ourselves. Now, back to what I was saying. This entire island has been in the Castor family for generations, but Hodge decided to build the retreat on it a dozen years ago."

"Hodge?" I asked her. She'd mentioned him by name earlier, but I wasn't at all sure that I'd heard it correctly.

"I know, it's unusual, right? H. J. quickly became Hodge when he was a kid, and that's what we all call him now." Cyn crinkled her nose as she explained, "Herman Julian is his given name; can you blame him? Anyway, back to the resort. We do a lot of corporate retreats, VIP getaways, and we've even had the entire island rented out by the month by a single person."

"Does that happen often?" I asked her.

"Most recently, we had a wealthy businessman from Europe stay with us. He spent his entire time alone walking the perimeter of the island collecting driftwood. It got so sparse that we had to put more out when he went to bed each night so he'd have more wood to discover and collect the next day."

"That must have really piled up in a month's time," I said, trying to imagine ever doing anything so eccentric.

"It never came to that, because he had a bonfire every night. All in all, he was one of the nicest guests I've ever met, and by the time he left, he was a changed man. Star has a way of doing that to some folks. They come tense and broken, and the place has a way of fixing them."

"How about the other people on the island now?" Jake asked.

I saw Cyn's lips purse for a second before she replied. "They're all fine, I'm sure. We've all mostly just met, but there are a few repeat visitors."

It was clear that our escort was lying about everything being fine, and I was comforted knowing that she wasn't very good at being deceitful. I began to wonder if Jake had been right after all to have misgivings about our offer out of the blue. What did we have in store for us?

"Is *everyone* here a prize winner?" I asked her.

Jake nodded his approval at my question, and I smiled at him. He was a crackerjack investigator, but it felt good reminding him every now and then that I had skills of my own.

"No, from what I understand, you're the only two who have never met the boss," Cyn said. "In fact, Hodge handled the invitations himself. Well, I'm sure that he handed them to Mrs. Bellacourt, and she took things from there." She said the woman's name as though it were draped in italics, and I wondered what her story was.

"Is she Hodge's romantic companion?" I ventured.

Cyn barked out in a burst of involuntary laughter for a moment before quickly squelching it. "Sorry about that. I'd appreciate it if you didn't mention that little outburst to anyone. I'm certain it wouldn't be appreciated by any of the people involved."

"You don't have to worry about us. Our lips are sealed," I said with a grin, and Jake nodded in agreement as well.

Cyn explained, "Mrs. Bellacourt is Hodge's personal assistant and has been for years. She not only travels everywhere with him, but she also handles everything short of nuclear launch codes for Hodge. Mrs. Bellacourt runs things with a firm hand, and I've yet to see anyone cross her and live to tell the tale."

"She sounds intriguing. I look forward to meeting her," I said.

Cyn's only reply was a guarded shrug.

"Since everyone else appears to know each other, could you give us any information about our fellow guests?" Jake asked.

"I didn't say that," Cyn corrected him. "*Hodge* knows each of them in his own way, but some of our guests clearly haven't met until today."

"But surely you can give us some basic information about them." Why was my husband so interested in who was sharing the island with us?

I was about to ask him just that when Cyn said, "Sorry. Only Hodge and Mrs. Bellacourt are at liberty to discuss our guests, but feel free to ask either one of them if you'd like." It was clear from her tone of voice that the subject was closed. After pausing for a moment, she continued her lecture. "The Star Island Retreat is made up of five cottages, each one located on a perimeter point of the star. That's where the majority of our guests will be staying. In the center of the island, there's a nice main lodge called Star Burst, where the restaurant is located, as well as a grand communal gathering place, some smaller meeting rooms, a few other emergency guest rooms, and a compact infirmary just off the kitchen area."

"Where does Hodge stay when he's on the island?" Jake asked.

"His suite is on the top floor of the lodge, but to my knowledge, no visitor to the resort has ever been invited up there, so I wouldn't get my hopes up for seeing it if I were you."

"And the staff?" I asked. "Do you all stay in cottages as well?"

"No, ma'am. Our accommodations are in the basement of the lodge. That area is officially known as Star Dust, but we affectionately call it the Swamp among ourselves," she said. "All five cottages are occupied this extended weekend, and two of the rooms at the lodge are taken as well. Hodge is on the island at the moment, so he'll be in his suite, naturally. All in all, we have a full house."

"How many staff members are in residence here?" I asked as I got a better glimpse of the island. The trees that inundated the shoreline looked lovely with their snowy trappings, and the dock we were heading toward had a nice dusting as well, though as I watched, a husky young man was busy shoveling the accumulations off into the water, undoubtedly just for us.

"We usually have seven staff members on hand at any given moment, but right now, we're down to four."

"Who's that currently shoveling snow off the dock?" Jake asked.

"That's Harley. He's been clearing snow all day around the property, and he handles just about anything that requires brute force around here. Choonie is our cook and chief bottle washer, and that just leaves Nan and me. We're the maids, chauffeurs, servers, and whatever other jobs are needed inside. We're always hopping, but I'd rather be busy myself if there's a choice."

"Harley must be freezing if he's been out all day shoveling snow," I remarked.

Cyn grinned. "Don't feel *too* sorry for him. The guy's made of tough stock, and he loves being outside in the cold. You can't see it, but he has a wetsuit on under those clothes. He can't shut up about training for some kind of polar bear swim the second we're cut free from this weekend assignment. I've caught him swimming in the lake like a madman more than once since it turned so cold. Who in his right mind would do that in this kind of weather? Personally, I think he's bonkers."

"I'm sure we each have idiosyncrasies no one else understands," Jake said.

"Maybe," she conceded, though just barely.

"Wow, it sounds like a lot of work for just four people," I said.

"Don't you worry about us. We'll manage just fine," Cyn said. "Besides, this is the end of our season, and you are our last guests. Now, back to the lecture. I need to speed it up since we're almost there. There are lots of paths and hiking trails around the island, so feel free to explore. Altogether, we have a little over four acres, and with the exception of the Swamp and the penthouse, it's all at your disposal. Oh, one more thing. Cell phones are useless on the island, so there's no use even trying, and there are no landlines here, either. This place is as isolated as you can get in this modern age of universal connectivity."

"Isn't it dangerous to be that inaccessible?" Jake asked her.

"Not as much as you might think. Besides this boat, which is made of stouter stuff than it might look, there's a short-wave radio for emergencies. Don't worry. You're both going to be in good hands here. I promise."

"What do your parents think about you being so isolated out here?" I asked her, probably overstepping my bounds, but I'd already grown to genuinely like this young lady, and it seemed to be in my nature to worry about her and others I'd taken under my wing from time to time and not just Emma Blake, my assistant.

"I lost my mother just before I got this job, and I never knew my father. As far as I'm concerned, it's just me."

"I'm so sorry," I said, feeling an overwhelming amount of

19

sympathy for the young woman. What would it be like to be without family? I couldn't imagine it. Not only did I have Jake, but my mother still played an important part in my life, even at her extended age.

"Don't worry about me," Cyn said with a soft smile. "Mom had a good life, though it was much too short for me. As for my dad, who's to say? It's hard to miss something you've never had. Mom loved to tell me stories about how my father was someone rich and powerful who couldn't be with us, but they were just fairytales she told me at bedtime, as far as I'm concerned. Being on my own is just a part of who I am." As Cyn said the last bit, she docked the boat, casting a line to Harley, who deftly plucked it out of the air and secured it with more grace than I'd expected from the big man. Clearly he'd noticed us coming in and had tarried to help us tie up the boat.

"Welcome to the Star," Harley said gruffly as he steadied the small craft for us to allow us to climb out, each in our own turn.

"Thanks," I said as I stuck out a hand. "I'm Suzanne, and this is Jake."

The young man showed no reaction to my informality as he shook my hand for the briefest of moments before letting it go, doing the same with Jake as well. Cyn had been right about at least one thing: I could see the edge of a wetsuit under his jacket.

"Bags?" he asked Cyn as he looked completely past us and turned his attention to our captain.

She tossed them to Harley, who then immediately started up the path; with or without us, he clearly didn't care.

As Harley hurried away, he asked over his shoulder, "Light, right?"

"That is correct, sir," Cyn said as she joined us on the dock.

"Light?" I asked.

"It's just some of Hodge's quirky sense of humor. The guest

cabins are called Star Light, Star Bright, Star Shine, Star Gaze, and Star Fire."

"And your place in the basement is called the Swamp?" Jake asked with a smile.

"Remember, it's officially named Star Dust, but we just call it the Swamp. I'll leave the reason why it earned that name up to your imagination."

"I'm curious about the main lodge," I said. "Earlier, you referred to it as Star Burst. Is there a reason for that?"

"Yes. It was built on the direct center of the island, and all points radiate out from it, just like a starburst," Cyn said. "Harley is taking your things directly to Light, but we need to get you two to the lodge first, or Star Burst, if you prefer, though everyone around here just calls it the lodge. There's a get-together in about ten minutes, and believe me, you don't want to miss that. The island is so small, it will be good to meet everyone at the beginning, so there won't be any awkward introductions later on. Just follow me."

"You're in charge," Jake said with a slight shrug. "Lead on."

I took his hand in mine as we walked and whispered, "Isn't this exciting?"

"Let's just hope this is as exciting as it gets," he replied.

Did he have a gut feeling that things were about to get immediately worse, or was it just a part of his general mood?

Either way, I had a feeling myself that we were about to find out.

CHAPTER 3

I
F THE COTTAGES WERE ANYTHING like the main lodge,
they were bound to be spectacular. We finished walking the
uphill path and came upon a massive structure reminiscent
of the great North Woods lodges of the past. Thick, dark stained
logs made up the exterior, broken up only by expansive areas
of glass that no doubt offered spectacular views of all of the
surrounding beauty. The roof had been topped with dark-
green metal, making it blend into the surrounding canopy of
evergreens, and several large boulders were strewn around the
structure as well. The building as a whole looked as though it
had sprung up from the ground, complete, rather than being
built upon it, and if I hadn't known its age, I would have guessed
that it had been there for at least two hundred years.

"Wow," was all that I could manage to say at first.

Cyn nodded in agreement. "It's pretty amazing, isn't it? I
have the same reaction myself every time I walk up the hill and
see the lodge in all of its glory, and you know what? It never
gets old."

"And you say that one family owns this entire island and all
of the structures on it?" Jake asked as we approached the front
of the lodge and headed straight for a set of massive wooden
doors that had been stained to match the exterior. The hardware
was all hand-wrought iron, and it added its own sense of gravity
to the building. I noticed that the door handle and hinges had
all been embellished with small feather designs within rather

graceful and intricate designs, and I realized this place must have cost a fortune to build.

"One *man*, actually. As far as I know, Hodge is nearly the last remaining member of his entire clan. With the single exception of Molly Rider, who happens to be here this weekend as well, apparently he has no heirs at all."

"Does that mean that she gets all of this once he's gone?" I asked, not considering how crass it must have sounded until I'd heard myself speak the words. "Strike that. It's none of my business."

Cyn shrugged. "Feel free to speculate about what happens to it all once he's gone. Everyone else around Hodge does, but if you ask me, I doubt that she'll be getting much of an inheritance. He and Molly don't exactly see eye to eye on a great many things, and she seems to be a constant source of irritation for him." Cyn frowned. "Okay, I definitely shouldn't have said that. What is it about you, Suzanne? I've known you less than fifteen minutes, and yet here I am telling you all of our secrets."

"She's easy to talk to," Jake said with a nod.

"Maybe a little too easy. I need to be a little more careful about what I say."

"We'd never tell anyone about this conversation, or any we may have with you. You have to understand our curiosity, given the grandeur of this place. Surely he has a plan in place for his ultimate demise," Jake said.

"If he does, he hasn't chosen to share it with me," she said offhandedly. It was clear that Cyn had overstepped her bounds and now regretted it. She was almost brusque as she instructed us, "Now, if you'll go on inside, someone will announce the meeting soon. I've got work to do to prepare for this evening's meal."

Another young woman approached us before Cyn could break away, and I saw by her nametag that she was Nan, the other maid/waitress/staffer, though she didn't identify herself as such to us. After a brief whispered conversation between them, Nan took a step back and waited as Cyn turned back to us before we could get inside.

"I'm afraid there's been a change of plans," she said with a heavy frown, clearly troubled by some new development.

"They haven't canceled our visit, have they?" I asked, suddenly saddened by the prospect of going back to April Springs without getting to experience this place. "I'd be so disappointed if we didn't get a chance to stay here on the island."

"To the contrary. Apparently Hodge would like to see you both in his apartment before you meet the rest of this weekend's guests."

I looked at Cyn for a moment before I spoke. "I thought you said that we'd never see that part of the lodge while we were here," I said.

"Don't ask me; I'm just as surprised as you are. You're the first ones who've ever been invited there since I've been on staff over the past three years, and we've had several major CEOs and foreign dignitaries stay with us during that time who begged for an audience with Hodge, only to be rebuffed." Cyn looked at us, clearly wondering what made us so special.

There was no reason to ask me: I didn't have a clue myself.

"If you'll follow me," Nan said after introducing herself to us and escorting us directly to what appeared to be a blank wall just inside the main entry. I got only a glimpse of the main room with its massive stone fireplace and its comfortable couches before a hidden panel opened in front of us and we were whisked upstairs in a private elevator.

"How did you do that?" I asked her, marveling at how the panel had silently slid away upon our approach.

"It's sweet, isn't it?" Nan asked. "The elevator is coded to recognize only certain staff by their thumbprints, and Hodge too, of course. If you'll look carefully later, you'll see that one knot on the paneling near the elevator door doesn't look anything like the others. If your thumbprint isn't coded in, you just stand there in front of a blank wall waiting for something to happen, and it never will."

We rode up together in silence, and the door finally opened straight into a massive space. It appeared that most of the top floor was taken up by one large room, featuring its own cozy fireplace surrounded by several comfortable chairs and couches. There were no kitchens, bedrooms, offices, or even bathrooms in sight, but after seeing the entrance to the elevator, it wouldn't have surprised me to learn that they were all there as well, hidden behind panels of their own. Whoever had decorated the space had stayed true to the floor below, and I wondered yet again how any one person could own it all.

Jake and I stepped out of the elevator together, but Nan stayed just inside. "Hodge will be with you shortly," she said.

"Aren't you coming in, too?" I asked her.

"No, my clearance covers only the elevator, not the main living space up here," she said as the door closed softly between us.

I looked around in awe as Jake whistled softly beside me before he said, "Would you check out that view."

We both walked over to the main expanse of windows and took in our surroundings. From our elevation, we could make out the water that surrounded us on all sides through the treetops, including the dock we'd so recently landed at, and the paths that led to each cottage through the trees. We couldn't see a great deal of definition or detail of the other structures, but there were small cleared areas around each cottage that allowed us to at least get a flavor of them. In some ways, it felt as though we were viewing some kind of miraculous computer rendering, but it was all clearly real enough. In the direct center of this isolated island, we were on top of our own little world as we took in everything within the panoramic view.

"It's quite breathtaking, isn't it?" a man directly behind us asked.

I hadn't even heard him enter the room. "H. J. Castor, I presume," Jake said coolly. He hadn't liked being taken off guard any more than I had.

"Everybody just calls me Hodge," the man said as he extended a massive hand to us. Our host looked more like a rugged outdoorsman than he did a multimillionaire. I guessed that he was somewhere in his late fifties, with graying temples that were in stark contrast to the full head of jet-black hair above. There was a faded strawberry birthmark near his right ear and a scar along his chin that showed that this man hadn't always lived a pampered and luxurious lifestyle. He was a shade under six feet tall, and if I had to guess, I'd say he weighed somewhere around two hundred and fifty pounds, without much fat on him. In fact, Hodge Castor looked as though he could have been carved from one of the logs that made up his lodge, and I pitied the unfortunate foe who was delusional enough to challenge him to a fight. "Welcome to Star Island."

"This is quite an impressive place you've got," I said. "We're honored to have won your contest."

Hodge frowned for a moment before he spoke, as though he was considering his options of answering, and then he finally said, "About that."

"You're canceling our stay, aren't you?" I asked unhappily for the second time in ten minutes. Why else would we be meeting the owner so soon upon our arrival?

"What? No, of course not. Whatever gave you that idea?" Hodge asked, clearly surprised by my question.

"If not that, then why have we been summoned up here? I understand this is a hard invitation to get, and I can't imagine that you invite *all* of your prizewinners into your inner sanctum," Jake said.

"There *are* no prizewinners," Hodge said. "That was merely a ruse to get you both to the resort. You were the only guests presented with the concept of winning anything. The rest have been invited directly by me. Some of our visitors believe they are on a corporate retreat for my organization, while others think this weekend is a show of gratitude for past favors done me, but they're all wrong about why I gathered them here. I felt it best to couch my request for your presence in a way that would be more palatable to you than a simple appeal to your better natures."

Jake nodded as he frowned at the news. "I wish that I could say I'm surprised, but in all honesty, I suspected as much from the start. Now, if you'll excuse us, my wife and I need to get back to April Springs before the snow makes the roads impassable."

I wanted more information myself, but Jake was right. It turned out that there *was* something fishy about the whole thing, and we'd be better off getting away from the island while we still could.

"Would you at least do me the courtesy of hearing me out first?" he asked. "If, after you've heard what I have to say, you still want to leave, I'll make sure you're off the island in plenty of time to get back home tonight."

It was clear that Hodge wasn't used to being refused any request, but then again, he hadn't met us. "Mr. Castor, you heard my husband. There's no excuse for subterfuge. We're leaving."

Hodge frowned in frustration, and then he asked, "If you won't hear me out on my account, how about doing it as a favor for an old friend?"

Jake asked softly, "I'm afraid that we don't know you, sir, so how can you be an old friend of either one of us?" I long ago realized that when my husband got both quiet and polite, trouble was not far away. It was as effective as a rattlesnake's warning to anyone who knew him, and no one could dismiss the combination without dire consequences, no matter how rich they might be.

"I'm not talking about the three of us, but you're friends with George Morris, and he's the one who suggested I bring you both here in the first place."

Suddenly, everything changed.

Bringing our old friend into the conversation was another matter altogether.

"How do you know George?" I asked him.

"We've been friends for twenty years," Hodge said. "Would you at least sit with me while I explain?"

"I don't see what it could hurt," I said, even though Jake had been about to refuse the request. My husband was the only person I knew, with the possible exception of my mother, who could be more stubborn than I was, but I honestly wanted to see what Hodge had to say for himself. There would always be time to leave later. At least that was what I kept telling myself.

Jake reluctantly joined me in front of the fireplace, where a nice blaze was burning steadily away. "Go on. You have our attention. Tell us how you know George Morris," Jake prompted our host once we were all seated.

"I was in Charlotte twenty years ago for a meeting with a group of what I thought were foreign investors interested in one of my projects. My security team hired some freelance support— moonlighting cops, that sort of thing—and George was one of the folks they hired. The deal was all a ruse for a kidnapping attempt, and George was the only one who figured it out in time. He got me out of a very dicey situation, and we've been friends ever since."

"I'm guessing we're here for some reason besides the fact that George helped you twenty years ago," Jake said. "This invitation wasn't extended out of gratitude for any past service he might have provided for you."

Hodge smiled. "George was right. You two really *are* the real deal. No, I needed help again, so I turned to George. There's an old saying, *Help a man out, and the next time he's in trouble, he'll remember you again.* Not very flattering, is it? Anyway, George recommended that I contact the two of you. He wanted to tell you what it was about, but I asked him not to say anything directly to you until I could make contact myself."

I smiled. "You'll be happy to know that he lived up to his part of the bargain." I turned to Jake and said, "I wondered why George was lingering around the donut shop this morning." Then, looking at Hodge again, I continued, "He was there when your invitation arrived, and he kept prompting me to open it in his presence. I'm sure that he wanted me to read it so he could explain the situation, but I didn't follow the script he must have written in his mind. Now I know why. He wasn't going to be the one who brought it up, but by being there on hand, he'd be available for consultation, so that way he wouldn't be violating your trust, or ours, either. I thwarted that plan purely by accident by refusing to open the envelope in his presence. No wonder he seemed so frustrated with me."

"That sounds like something he'd do," Hodge agreed.

"So then, we are here for our sleuthing skills," Jake said heavily. "Pardon me for stating the obvious, but you're a very rich man, sir. Why would you need to turn to a retired cop and a donutmaker for help, with the wealth at your disposal?"

"You're rather blunt, aren't you?" Hodge asked Jake.

"I prefer to think of it as being direct."

"I can live with that," Hodge said with a grudging nod. "The fact is that I can't trust anyone around me, not even Belle."

"Is that honestly Mrs. Bellacourt's first name?" I asked

him. "She must have really loved her husband to become Belle Bellacourt."

"No, Belle is just my nickname for her," he told us with a bent grin. "She's my most trusted employee, and I like to think of her as a friend as well, but I just can't be sure of anyone at the moment. My inner circle is *all* suspect right now, so I need someone from the outside who can't be tagged as active law enforcement from the start, or anyone privy to the inner workings of my organization. If George says that I can trust you, then I know that I can. He's about the only person left on the planet that I *do* trust."

"How sad for you," I said without thinking.

"Yes, it is, isn't it?" Hodge asked a little wistfully.

"Suspected of what?" Jake persisted. "You just said that everyone close to you is suspect. Why?"

"Someone has recently made an attempt on my life, or three of them, if you prefer to think of them that way, and *whoever* it is, they are almost surely on Star Island right now with us."

CHAPTER 4

I HAD A MILLION FOLLOW-UP QUESTIONS, but Jake managed to summarize them all in two simple words. "Please explain."

Hodge sighed heavily, and then he stood abruptly. "I'm parched, and telling this is just going to make matters worse. Would either one of you like something to drink? The spring water on the island is famous in the area for its natural sweetness."

"Why not?" I asked.

Jake frowned at me, unhappy for the interruption, but here was where my expertise came into play. We needed Hodge to be relaxed around us, and it was clear that he required a moment to come to grips with the fact that he was about to share the death threat with us. If we pushed him right now, it would take three times as long to get the information from him, but a pause would allow him to collect his thoughts, and then we could move ahead and see what we were dealing with.

Hodge handed me a tumbler of liquid drawn from a crystal glass pitcher, and I took a tentative sip. The water was even more amazing than he'd promised, cold and clear, as sweet as a kiss, and vastly satisfying. If the man owned no other asset in the world but the source of this water, he would still be a very rich man indeed. "You need to try this, Jake."

"Thanks, but I'm not thirsty."

I held my glass out to him and kept smiling until he took it. My husband had learned early on that when it came to my requests, many times the path of least resistance was the best one to take. I watched his expression as he took a small sip, and then a large gulp. His smile was answer enough that he knew that I'd been right. "That's incredible."

Hodge nodded with a smile. "It is, isn't it? I never grow tired of it. Some families who've lived in this area for generations consider it an elixir, and the artesian well is kept under lock and key," he said as he poured a glass for Jake as well. After we all had been served and our host had returned to his seat, he explained, "I was at my secret getaway last week, a little cabin in the woods not that far from here. No one but those closest to me knows about it. I was going about my business when someone took three rapid shots at me: bam, bam, bam. Before you suggest it, you should know that it couldn't have been random, not given the way that it happened. You have to know exactly where this cabin is, and then go through quite a bit of trouble to get to it, it's so well hidden. If I hadn't hung my coat up to dry on the corner of a tall chair and propped my hat on top of it, I wouldn't be here right now. Two shots missed the jacket entirely, but the third went straight through the chest pocket, close enough to where my heart would have been if I'd been wearing it to kill me."

"May we see the jacket in question?" Jake asked.

"There's no need. It was struck with a .22 caliber rifle bullet, just like the other slugs I dug out of the wall. I don't have to tell you that it's not hard to get your hands on a .22 rifle around these parts, so we have to assume that any of my suspects could have done it, regardless of whether it was a man or a woman. Don't believe for one second that this incident had to be isolated to the men. My grandmother had buckshot in her hip until the day she died from two men trying to steal her chickens. She took a hit, and some shot even embedded itself in her shotgun stock, but she still managed to wound them both with return fire and ran them off for good. Anyone who calls women the weaker sex doesn't know what they're talking about. There's no doubt in my mind about one thing, though; those were shots meant to kill me. After my narrow escape, I knew I had to do something before the would-be killer had more success with their next attempt, so I used the premise of a free vacation or a corporate bonding experience to lure everyone here. Some of my guests are valued employees, while others have been close to me for years through other avenues, but each person invited has a close connection to me. They are the only ones I could imagine who might benefit from my demise, at least in their minds. It's no secret that I have no obvious heir with the exception of Molly Rider, a clearly unpleasant as well as unpopular choice that I've rejected time and time again, so if *anyone* were to benefit from my death, there is no doubt it would be at least one of the folks who are gathered here this weekend. Evidently whoever took those shots at me decided that they couldn't wait for my natural end to come, no matter how quickly it might come."

"Excuse me for saying so," I interrupted him, "but why would *anyone* believe they would inherit from you anytime soon if they didn't help matters along themselves? You look as though you'll live at least another thirty years."

He shrugged slightly before answering in a somber voice, "The truth of the matter is that appearances can be deceiving. According to the best doctors I've been able to consult, at the very best, I have less than twelve months left to live."

"I'm so sorry," I said, which was my immediate reaction. "Are you in any pain?"

Our host smiled gently. "No, but thank you for asking. I won't go into specifics, only to note that the good news, if there is any in this kind of situation, is that apparently I'll be able to function quite well until near the very end."

"Who all knows you are dying?" Jake asked him gently.

"A surprisingly small group, actually," he said.

"Everyone gathered here, I suppose," I guessed. "Since they each must qualify for the list."

"What list is that?" Hodge asked with a gentle smile. Was he actually enjoying the conversation, as macabre as it was?

"The list of suspects you've compiled in your mind. The attempt was clearly untraceable or we wouldn't be here, and the number of possibilities wouldn't be that large. The potential killer has to believe they are currently in line to inherit at least something from you, but that's not the whole story, is it?" I asked.

"Why do you ask that?" he replied, perhaps a tad condescendingly, but I decided to let that slide, given the circumstances.

"Because you're also about to make a big change in something in your life, whether it's your personal situation or your business status. My guess is that you're either getting married, or you're going to sell off all of your holdings, and soon. Are you perhaps planning on starting up a charitable foundation, or maybe a medical research facility to combat whatever it is that's afflicting you?"

I'd scored more than one direct hit with my guesses judging by Hodge's hardening expression. "Who have you been talking to?"

Jake spoke up in my defense before I could do it myself. "If you're implying that my wife has an inside source of information within your circle, I can assure you that you're mistaken. Suzanne has the most amazing ability of extrapolating scenarios based on the sketchiest of details."

It was quite a compliment, one that I accepted gladly with a smile. "So, which is it?"

"Well, I'm not getting married, if that helps eliminate one of the possibilities," he said with a wry grin. "I tried that twice, and it didn't work out either time. My ex-wives are both well provided for, and they benefit nothing from my demise, so they won't be joining us this weekend, thank the good Lord above for small favors. I wasn't in love with either one of them, even though I thought I was both times."

"I'm so sorry you never got to experience true love," I said, thinking what an empty life it would be without someone in it to care for so completely.

"Don't shed too many tears on my account. I've known love, just not with either of them. Unfortunately, happily-ever-after just wasn't meant to be, but I still think about her on dark and lonely nights," he said wistfully. "It was over twenty years ago, but sometimes it feels as though it were just yesterday."

Great. I'd managed to make a dying man feel even worse about his situation than he had before we'd spoken. "So, is the money going for a charitable foundation, or is it being poured into medical research?" I asked.

"My prognosis is assured, and not all that common, so that area holds little interest for me. I'm liquidating my assets beginning next week in order to fund the Wilderness and Wildlife Consortium. I've always loved being out in nature, and I want to preserve what I can for generations to come. It's the best legacy I could ask for, and about the only one left for me."

"I imagine none of the group gathered below is happy about the news," Jake said.

He nodded. "A few have feigned interest in my plans, but some have met the new direction with open contempt. Regardless of how they reacted, I can see the capacity within each of them to try to stop me while they still can."

"Do you have dossiers on your guests?" Jake asked him. "It would be extremely helpful to know something about them before we meet."

"Actually, I have rather extensive ones, but I'd rather you

treat them each without any prejudices or preconceptions you might get from what I've gathered myself," he said heavily.

"You do realize that you are putting our investigation at a disadvantage by withholding what might be valuable information to us," Jake said sternly.

"I'm afraid that's the way it has to be," Hodge said firmly. "I'm sure you're both wondering at this point what is in this for you."

I shot him a confused look. It was as though we'd been speaking English all along when he'd suddenly switched to Portuguese. "Pardon me?"

"Don't worry. I haven't forgotten about the two of you. I can assure you that I don't expect you to do this without getting anything in return. You'll both be rewarded handsomely. I always pay those who do my bidding."

I stood, put my glass down on the table in front of me, and after signaling Jake, he followed suit. "What are you doing?" Hodge asked me, clearly caught off guard by our actions.

"We're leaving," I said with a hint of sadness in my voice. "Are you coming, Jake?"

"I'm right behind you," my husband said, and I couldn't have been more proud of him than I was at that moment.

Hodge stood as well, looking thoroughly confused by the situation. "I don't understand. What did I say?"

"How long has it been since you've had an interaction with someone who wasn't after your money or your influence? My guess is that it's been a long time. You act as though we can be bought or sold at your whim. I'm sorry, but we don't work that way," I said as I searched for the hidden elevator door. "How do you activate this blasted thing again?"

"Then you won't help me?" Hodge asked, for the first time sounding truly desperate.

"Let me ask you something," I said as I turned to face him. "Did George charge you anything extra for saving your life?"

Hodge frowned. "No, and it wasn't from lack of trying on my part. That's what made us such good friends. I knew that he couldn't be bought."

"And what makes you think the two of us would be any different?" I asked him. "George recommended us to you, and you felt free to invoke his name to convince us to stay. We can help you, but not on a sliding pay scale. You are friends with George, and so are we. It's as simple as that. Don't get me wrong. We have nothing against money per se. If you commissioned me to make you a hundred dozen donuts for a party, I'd be ready to quote you a fair price that allowed me some profit as well."

"I get that," Hodge said, but I interrupted him before he could add anything to the thought.

"Let me finish. On the other hand, if I came along and saw you dangling on the edge of a cliff and I stopped to negotiate a price before I helped you up, then I'd never be able to look at myself in the mirror again."

"Is it too late to say that I'm sorry?" Hodge asked contritely. "I'm not defending my behavior, but you were right before. It's been a long time since someone did something for me without expecting payment for it."

"Has it perhaps been as long as when George refused you twenty years ago?" Jake asked softly.

"That sounds about right to me," Hodge said. "Please? Will you help me? I need you both. I'm not afraid of dying—well, not too much—but I can't stand knowing that someone close to me wants it to come sooner rather than later."

I considered myself a good judge of character, and it was clear to me that this man was sincere in both his apology and his request. "We'll stay," I said, glancing over at Jake, who nodded in agreement as well.

"Thank you," Hodge said, clearly relieved by our acceptance. He glanced at his watch, and then he said hurriedly, "This took longer than I expected it to. If you don't go right now, you're going to be late for the welcoming party."

"We keep trying to leave, but your elevator won't let us," I told him, smiling softly.

"You need clearance to summon the elevator at either entrance," he said as he swiped his thumb over what had appeared to be a void in the wood but was clearly much more.

"Couldn't that be considered kidnapping, holding us here against our wills?" I asked him as the elevator door slid silently open at his summons.

"I wouldn't know. I've never had guests up here before."

Jake and I stepped onto the elevator, but Hodge didn't join us.

"Aren't you coming?" I asked him.

"I'm afraid I need to rest," he said. "This illness, while not debilitating, is not without its own costs."

"Well, get some rest, and try not to worry. We'll do our best to help," I said.

"That's all that I can ask. Thank you both."

As the door began to slide shut, Jake and I said in unison, "You're welcome."

As we traveled to the main floor, I said, "You were right."

"About what?"

"About there being more to this than it first appeared. I'm sorry I got us into this mess."

"Are you kidding me? I wasn't all that excited about coming before, but now it's really got my interest piqued."

"You never were one for vacations, were you?" I asked him with a grin. "It's always the busman's holiday for you."

"What can I say? I'm a man of simple interests. Come on," he said as the door opened. "Let's go find ourselves a potential killer."

CHAPTER 5

A STERN OLDER WOMAN MET US at the elevator door before we could join the others milling about in the expansive lounge area of the central part of the lodge. "I was told to escort you personally into the main hall," she said. "My name is Annalise Bellacourt," she added without extending her hand to us. "I am Mr. Castor's personal assistant, so if you need anything during your stay, I've been instructed to see that it is arranged."

"It's nice to meet you, Annalise," I said without thinking.

A cloud formed on her brow at the mention of her first name. "It's Mrs. Bellacourt, actually," she corrected me icily.

"Mrs. Bellacourt it is, then," I said. "How long have you worked for Hodge?"

Evidently I had breached protocol yet again. "I'm not at all sure how that is relevant, but I have been an employee of Mr. Castor for several years. Now, if you'll follow me, I am to introduce you to our other guests."

"Lead on," I said, finally giving up on making a connection with the woman, and as I did, I shot a quick look at Jake. He was doing his best to suppress a smile, and I might have been mad at him if he hadn't looked so cute doing it. I wasn't a big fan of being thwarted.

There was no opportunity to sulk, though. It was time for our first introduction. "May I present Mr. Castor's personal attorney, Mr. Carl Wilson," she said as we approached a short, squat man in his fifties who was built along the lines of a fire hydrant. His suit had obviously been tailored for his particular physique, because it fit him perfectly, but underneath the material was clearly a solidly built man. "Mr. Wilson, this is Suzanne Hart and Jake Bishop."

After shaking our hands solidly, he studied us each for a moment before saying, "You don't work for Hodge." There was no question in it; in fact, it felt a little like an accusation.

Mrs. Bellacourt interceded before we could explain. "They are the winners of this year's prize drawing."

"Humph," Wilson said, clearly unimpressed with our status. "What exactly is it that you do, Bishop?"

"As a matter of fact, I'm between jobs at the moment," Jake said with a grin.

Wilson could barely mask his contempt as he turned to me. "You as well, I suppose?"

"Oh, no, I have a full-time job. I make donuts for a living," I said with a smile of my own. Either he was gruff by nature, or Carl Wilson was not very taken with either one of us.

The attorney dismissed us both with a fleeting look, and then I saw him glance over at a young man in his late twenties laughing nearby. There was enough venom in the look to melt steel, and I had to wonder what the history between them might be.

"If you'll excuse us, our latest arrivals need to meet everyone before dinner," Mrs. Bellacourt said.

"Of course," Wilson said, dismissing us with a single gesture. "Will Hodge be along soon? There's something I really must discuss with him, and it can't wait."

Mrs. Bellacourt simply pursed her lips without really answering.

He seemed to take the response in stride. No doubt he'd gone up against Mrs. Bellacourt in the past.

I wanted to say something to Jake about the attorney, but we were already making our way to the next introduction, and besides, the assistant was guiding us as though we were prize cows. To my surprise, it wasn't another business associate, at least I didn't think so, at least not based on the way she was dressed. Wearing a dowdy little number that would never be offered in Gabby Williams' elegant secondhand clothing shop, ReNEWed, she appeared to be somewhere in her early thirties, a long and lean woman with dishwater-blonde hair that was clearly her natural tint. Her facial features resembled a greyhound, long and narrow, and her eyes were far too close together, at least in my opinion. Mrs. Bellacourt stepped in again before we had to introduce ourselves. "May I present Mr. Castor's fourth cousin, Miss Molly Rider? Miss Rider, please say hello to Jake Bishop and Suzanne Hart, this year's contest winners."

"Good for you," Molly said before turning to Mrs. Bellacourt and smiling softly. "Mrs. Bellacourt, you know I prefer just plain old Molly." Turning back to us, she said with a hint of sadness in her voice, "I'm the only family poor Hodge has left. We need to stick together, since we're all there is of our particular branch of our family tree."

"Molly it is," the personal assistant said automatically. Clearly she'd been corrected about the woman's preferences before, but just as obviously, she wasn't about to change her behavior.

"It must be fabulous being related to such a powerful man," I said, trying to make conversation with the young woman.

"I don't know about that. I'm just glad we still have each other," Molly replied. "Mrs. Bellacourt, I don't mean to be pushy, but do you know when we are going to eat? I'm sure everyone is getting hungry."

"It will be soon, I assure you," Hodge's assistant said, and then she pulled us away to lead us to the laughing man we'd seen earlier. "May I present Mr. Barry Day, Mr. Castor's senior vice president in acquisitions? This is Suzanne Hart and Jake Bishop."

"Wow, I sound pretty impressive when you put it like that, Belle," he said with a clearly artificial smile.

The executive's personal assistant visibly flinched at the use of the nickname her employer preferred, but she didn't comment.

"That's quite a title you've got there," Jake said amiably.

"For one so young, you mean?" Day asked archly. "Believe me, I've earned every bit of it, and I've got the CV to back it up. I graduated Harvard at sixteen, Wharton Business School before my eighteenth birthday, and I've worked for Hodge for the past six years. Give me another year and I'll be running the place." He laughed at his own statement, something that seemed to be second nature for him, but no one else found it amusing.

Mrs. Bellacourt was about to say something when a woman in her seventies joined us. "Are you laughing at your own jokes again because no one else will, Barry?" she asked him sweetly.

"It's not my fault my humor's over everyone else's head, Christy," Day said with a frown.

"If only that were true," she said with a twinkle in her eye. The overweight woman sported pink and green streaks in her hair, and I liked her immediately, maybe because of the way she'd handled the brash young man, or perhaps because she was completely nonplussed and unapologetic about being dressed in a faded muumuu despite her surroundings, not to mention the outside temperature. "I'm Christy Locke," she said as she offered us each her hand before proper introductions could be made.

"I'm Suzanne, and this is Jake," I said warmly.

"Ah, the contest winners. How delightful."

"How do you know Hodge?" Jake asked her pleasantly enough.

"Oh, we go way back," she said with a grin. "As a matter of fact, I gave him the stake to start up his first business."

I couldn't help myself. I whistled softly, and then I said, "Wow, you must be worth a fortune by now."

"You'd think so, wouldn't you? Alas, I let Hodge buy me almost completely out at far too cheap a price years ago, and I've never stopped regretting it. Oh well, at this point it's just water over the dam, and all of that."

"I believe it's under the bridge," Day corrected her.

"Under, over, dams, bridges, does any of it really matter?" She looked around the room and was clearly troubled by something. "Mrs. B, have you seen London lately?"

"The city's vastly overrated, if you ask me," Day said.

"I'm talking about the man, not the city, and you're wrong on that count as well. If you don't enjoy London, England, it's because you lack imagination, dear boy. London Peale and I were having the most interesting conversation about Scotland when I first arrived, but I haven't seen him in ages."

Mrs. Bellacourt studied the room for a moment, and then she said, "It appears that Mr. Peale has stepped out. I know for a fact that he was here twenty minutes ago."

"Maybe he's with Hodge up in the penthouse," she said.

"No, he's not there," I said without thinking about what I had just admitted.

That got the attention of everyone around us.

"You've already met Hodge?" Day asked.

"Wow, you must be more than meets the eye," Christy said.

Carl Wilson didn't comment, but I noticed that he'd been eavesdropping, and the news hadn't gone unnoticed.

Mrs. Bellacourt saved us from further speculation. "Contest winners always get an audience with Mr. Castor," she said, though I doubted that was anything near the truth, given the fact that there hadn't been a contest at all. Then again, since we were the only supposed winners there had ever been, maybe she was telling the literal truth after all. "Excuse me one moment, will you?" she asked as she motioned to Harley, who was standing uncomfortably to one side.

The staff employee approached us, his head held low.

"Harley, would you please visit Star Gaze and tell Mr. Peale that dinner will be served soon? I'm sure he wouldn't want to miss dinner."

"Neither would I, if it's ever served," Christy said. "It's been a long time since lunch. Will we be dining soon?"

"Very soon," Hodge's assistant said. "Now, if you'll excuse me, I need to make an announcement, and then we can dine." Mrs. Bellacourt moved to the front of the room, and by her mere presence, she managed to capture everyone's attention almost immediately. The woman was clearly a force to be reckoned with.

"Ladies and gentlemen, welcome to the Star Island Retreat! Mr. Castor sends his regrets, but he is occupied with an important matter upstairs, and thus he will be unavailable to join us at this time. No worries, though. He looks forward to catching up with each of you in the morning."

There were more than a few grumbles from the crowd, and I had to wonder if the reason most folks had come to the island in the first place was to see Hodge, whether to enjoy his company or make another attempt on his life, I couldn't say. I had a hard time visualizing any of these people shooting at him in the woods. Then again, Barry Day might do it if he thought his plans for conquering the world before he turned thirty were being thwarted. I could also imagine Carl Wilson taking those careful shots. He looked as though he'd have no compunctions about eliminating *anything* that caused him displeasure. Molly Rider was a bit of a stretch, but if she thought she'd inherit the bulk of his estate upon the man's demise—no matter how much he'd claimed to protest otherwise—she might be willing to go out of her comfort zone to expedite the process. Christy Locke seemed bitter about losing out on untold wealth by jumping the gun liquidating her stock, so maybe she resented Hodge's move more than she let on. That left London Peale. I didn't know his story, but his absence was suspicious by its very nature. Where could he have gone, and what was he up to? The questions kept rattling around in my head as Mrs. Bellacourt continued speaking.

"Never fear, he has promised me that he will make himself available to us all tomorrow. In the meantime, I am to instruct you all before dinner that this extended weekend will be full of food, fun, and activities. Mr. Castor has planned quite an experience for you all. There are activity packets waiting for you in your respective lodgings, but the first event will take place here, immediately following dinner. When you're finished with your meals, please meet back here for your initial experience of the weekend." She pursed her lips as she saw Barry Day about to comment, and she quickly added, "Of course, you're under no obligation to participate, but you should know that Mr. Castor would greatly appreciate you all taking part, and he wanted me to personally convey that message to each of you. I'm sure you'll all be delighted in seeing what's in store for you."

Mrs. Bellacourt nodded to Cyn, who was standing near a set of double doors along one wall. She took her cue and rang a small silver bell as the doors opened. "Dinner is now served," she announced, and we all headed in together, with the only absence being the mysterious London Peale, and Harley, the worker who'd been sent to fetch him. I expected Mr. Peale to show up soon, but in the meantime, we had plenty of suspects to interrogate, albeit delicately, since no one knew the real reason that Jake and I were there.

"I wonder what we're having for dinner?" I asked my husband softly as we walked into the dining room together.

"I have no idea, but I'm sure it will be tasty," he replied.

"At least I hope so. If they serve sushi, I'm stealing the boat and heading back to shore."

I looked around the dining room, and I was surprised to find that it had been outfitted more like a restaurant in town than a rustic lodge. For some reason, I'd been expecting to see one long table where food would be served family style, passed between the guests and enjoyed by all in a communal setting. Instead, there were small tables of four spread throughout the room. There was a distinct lack of charm in the seating arrangements, as far as I was concerned. Another massive stone fireplace in one corner offered a nice blaze, and there were large expanses of open windows on three sides, all of which were dark at the moment.

Apparently, night fell quickly, and heavily, on the island.

I was going to steer Jake toward the table where Barry Day and Molly Rider were about to sit, but then I saw the placeholders already resting at each spot.

Apparently we were to be seated with Mrs. Bellacourt, not my first choice by any stretch of the imagination, and not because of her lack of a sparkling personality. We were there to mingle with our suspects, not the staff. "Are these seating assignments firm?" I asked her.

"I'm afraid so. Mr. Castor gave strict instructions that no one was to deviate from his assignments," she intoned in a voice that dared not be challenged.

So much for adding to our investigation with some subtle questioning.

At least we were going to get to eat.

I just hoped that it wasn't sushi myself.

Cyn and Nan moved rhythmically among the widespread tables

with practiced ease, and Cyn even managed to wink at me once when Mrs. Bellacourt wasn't looking. The initial salads were delightful, and after they were taken away, we were given the choice of prime rib, glazed chicken, or salmon. "How can the chef prepare enough food to give us all those choices?" I asked her.

"It's easy. The staff gets the leftovers," she said with a grin.

"Ahem," Mrs. Bellacourt said stiffly, and Cyn nodded her acceptance of the soft rebuke.

"I'll have the prime rib," I said after a moment's pause.

"Make that two," Jake added.

"Nothing for me, thank you," Mrs. Bellacourt said. She had barely tasted her salad, so her refusal surprised me.

"You're not going to eat?" I asked her, incredulous that anyone would pass up a chance to be waited on and served what had to be a delicious entree.

"I make it a habit to eat sparingly at the end of the day," she said, losing just about all of the meager affection I'd managed to generate for her so far. What a ridiculous notion! My attitude was to eat when you get the opportunity, because you never know when your next meal might be. Granted, that philosophy had served to pack on a few more pounds than I needed to carry around with me, but it was still a sound principle in my mind.

"Aren't there any vegan choices?" Molly Rider asked Nan gently. "Hodge knows about my dietary restrictions." With a soft frown, speaking in a voice that I was barely able to hear from our table, she added, "Meat is murder, you know."

"Sure it is, but it's tasty, tasty murder," Barry Day intoned.

No one laughed, but that was par for the course for Barry's humor, or lack thereof.

"If it's not too much trouble, I'd love a baked potato," Molly asked her server.

"Of course. What would you like on it?" Nan asked.

"I'm sure that this is going to sound crazy to you, but I want one plain."

"Plain?" Nan asked skeptically.

"Yes, plain, please: no butter, no sour cream, no toppings," she said. "That's just the way I like them. Once you taste the potato in all of its glory, you'll never go back to disguising its flavor with unnecessary extras."

"I didn't think they had *any* flavor by themselves," Barry said, trying to joke again, without success.

"Yes, ma'am. I'm sure we can do that," Nan said, doing her best not to smile. Evidently she found Barry Day's humor more appealing than I did, but I had to wonder if it was more because of his status in life than his comedic material. Barry caught her open glance at him, and I could almost see the gears turning in his head, weighing the chance to score points with the server versus the prospect of offending his boss somehow. Evidently it didn't take long for his pragmatic side to win, and he was quite subdued as he placed his own order in a monotone without making eye contact.

Nan nearly faltered, the dismissal was so complete, but she quickly caught herself and moved on to the last table.

I glanced over and saw that Carl Wilson and Christy Locke were in deep conversation about something, but the moment they noticed me looking their way, it ended abruptly. What was going on between the two of them? Had they just been exchanging inane pleasantries, or was there something more ominous going on there? If they *were* conspiring about something, they would be two of the oddest cohorts I'd ever seen in my life.

The rest of the entrée orders were taken without incident, and we were served not very long after. The staff would indeed be dining well, at least tonight, if they'd be feasting on the items that hadn't been selected by the guests. After everyone else was served, Nan walked past us with the biggest baked potato I'd ever seen in my life, as naked as the moment it had been pulled from the earth. I loved potatoes just about every way imaginable, including a potato donut I'd developed over the years, but I wasn't sure that I'd ever had one all by itself. Molly seemed delighted, though. She dug in to her potato with such gusto that I was impressed with the joy she took from what couldn't be an easy lifestyle choice in this era of meat-loving carnivores.

The prime rib steaks were even more amazing than I could have imagined, served with sides of creamed spinach, garlic mashed potatoes, and what had to be fresh homemade bread. Cyn moved around the room offering wine, which we all enjoyed, and I settled in to one of the best meals I'd ever had in my life.

It was a good thing the food was so amazing; the conversation with Mrs. Bellacourt was filled with our elaborate questions answered with her nearly monosyllabic responses. It was more than a little off-putting to be dining on such a fine meal while she sat there occasionally sipping from her water glass. I was willing to bet that it wasn't even water from the spring Hodge had shared with us earlier. That would be too decadent for the woman, I imagined.

I finally gave up on Mrs. Bellacourt and turned to Jake. "It's really pretty amazing, isn't it?"

"It's all perfect," he said as he set his fork down for the final time, since his plate was now empty. "I wonder what we're having for dessert."

He'd just put away enough food to placate a teenage boy, but the man was still interested in satisfying his sweet tooth as well.

"Can you really hold another bite?" I asked him.

"Try me," he said with a laugh.

Cyn came by to refill our water glasses, so I seized the opportunity to quiz her.

"Is there any chance we're getting dessert tonight as well?" I asked her. "Before you judge me, you should know that I'm only asking for my husband."

"Sure you are," Jake said with a smile. The meal had clearly improved his mood immensely, and I for one was happy to see it. We might be on a working holiday of sorts, but it was nice that he had the opportunity to relax a little as well.

"There's chocolate mousse, and berries with cream."

"Don't you dare say both," I warned him before he could answer.

"Fine. The mousse sounds perfect," he said. "What are you going to have, Suzanne?"

I didn't need the extra calories, but then again, I might never get this particular opportunity again. "Why not? Make it two. Care to join us, Mrs. Bellacourt?"

"Thank you, but no. I must see to something in the kitchen. If you'll excuse me?"

"Of course," I said, and in a moment, she was gone.

"Wow, she's deceptively light on her feet, isn't she?" Jake asked.

"You don't know the half of it," our server said. "That woman can materialize out of thin air when she wants to. She scares me a little, just between the three of us."

"I'm sure she works hard to cultivate that fear," I said. "It's one way of dealing with the staff under her."

"I'm willing to bet that you don't do that with your employees," Cyn said.

"I just have the one, and I have to admit, she's more of a friend and surrogate daughter to me than an employee."

Cyn nodded in approval. "I'm not surprised to hear that at all. Two chocolate mousses, coming right up. Or should that be chocolate moussi?"

Jake pondered it for a moment before responding. "Well, since the plural of a regular moose is still moose, let's say mousse is a good plural as well. Nobody wants to say mousses. It just sounds silly."

"That's a fair point," Cyn said, laughing a little. "Whatever you'd like to call them, I'll have two here in a shake."

After Cyn retreated into the kitchen to fetch our desserts, I asked Jake, "Is it just me, or is she way too clever and personable to be doing this for a living?"

"There's nothing wrong with serving and waiting on people," Jake said.

"Don't you think I know that? I spend half my life serving my customers. I just mean Cyn seems to have a great deal on the ball."

"I don't doubt it. Would you expect Hodge to hire anyone less? For all we know, she's between semesters at Harvard Law," Jake said.

"You're right. Just because she's working here at the moment doesn't mean that she can't be brilliant as well. Harley, on the other hand, seems to have peaked, as far as I can tell."

I looked over at the brooding young bruiser, who'd returned to the dining room without London Peale. He was doing his best to ignore all of us and was currently studying one of his own thumbnails intently.

"What's wrong? Don't you like the strong, silent type?" Jake asked me with a slight smile.

"I do, but I like a dash of intelligence thrown in as well."

"I'm honored," he said with a slight nod of the head.

"You should be. After all, I don't marry just anybody."

"And for that, I am eternally grateful," he replied. We'd each been married before we'd met to other people, but both relationships had ended badly. My husband had cheated on me with a hairdresser, while Jake had lost his wife through tragedy. Still, the fact that we'd found each other, and as a direct result of a murder investigation no less, made it that much more special to me.

Cyn came back quickly with our desserts as promised, and then she asked, "May I get you anything else?"

"No, thank you. This has all been perfect," I said as I eyed the mousse in front of me. I should have asked for one so Jake and I could have split it, but if it tasted half as good as it looked, there wouldn't be much left of it soon anyway.

I was right.

The mousse was incredible, and before I knew it, my spoon was scraping the bottom of the serving dish. Somehow it was all gone, though I had no immediate recollection of consuming it so rapidly.

Mrs. Bellacourt reentered the dining room, but instead of returning directly to us, she found Harley and said something softly to him. He shook his head in the negative, and after a moment's whispered instructions, he headed out the back door.

When she rejoined us, Jake asked her, "Is there a problem?"

"No, I'm sure it's nothing."

My husband wasn't about to accept that as an answer. "Mrs. Bellacourt, Mr. Castor gave us full access to any information we might need this weekend. Now, I'll ask you once again. Is something wrong?"

Our host's personal assistant didn't look happy, but after the way Jake stated it, she really had no choice but to tell us the truth.

"I'm afraid that Mr. Peale is still missing, and I can't imagine where he's wandered off to."

CHAPTER 6

"WHAT DO YOU MEAN, HE'S missing?" Jake asked. "Surely this island isn't so large that it can't be searched easily enough."

"You'd be surprised," Mrs. Bellacourt replied. "The trees are rather dense in some places, and added to that, we've got snow on the ground as well as near-total darkness outside. There's supposed to be a nearly full moon tonight, but at the moment, the clouds are obscuring all but a little of its light. If Mr. Peale has wandered off somewhere alone, he could be in for a very bad night of it. The temperature is supposed to drop down into the teens, and I'm afraid of what might happen to him if he doesn't show up soon."

"Could he have left the island altogether?" I asked her.

"No, that's impossible. The only way on or off Star Island at the moment is via our skiff, and Harley just confirmed that it's safely tied up at the dock."

"Surely there are other boats on the water," I said. "Hodge can't own all of the land surrounding the lake as well, can he? Someone could have picked London up from the mainland without anyone realizing that he was even leaving."

"That's highly unlikely," Mrs. Bellacourt said firmly. "Mr. Castor owns the lake in its entirety, and many acres surrounding it. If someone brought a boat to the island, it would have to have been done without Mr. Castor's knowledge or approval."

"Then we need to form a search party immediately," Jake said as he stood. "Harley isn't going to be able to cover much ground alone. We should enlist everyone, arm them with flashlights, and send them out in pairs to search for the man until he's been found."

"I'm afraid that I can't authorize you to do that," Mrs. Bellacourt said icily, using a voice of command that I was certain was quite effective on her underlings.

Her only problem was that Jake wasn't a member of her staff.

"I apologize for the confusion. You misunderstood me. I wasn't asking you for your permission, I was simply telling you what we were going to do," Jake said.

My husband was about to head out into the meeting area of the lodge to retrieve his jacket when the dining room door opened and our host suddenly appeared.

It seemed that Hodge had decided to join us that night after all.

I had to wonder what had made our host change his plans so abruptly. Was it a whim, or had he been monitoring our conversations from upstairs all along? If so, had he decided to thwart Jake's plan of organizing search parties? *Was* the dining room bugged? If that were possible, what about other spots in the lodge? The cottages? How about the entire island? I didn't like the way my paranoia was manifesting itself, but what choice did I have? Hodge's timing was just a little too much of a coincidence for my taste.

"Friends, it's so good of you all to join me," our host said, doing his best to smile warmly at everyone gathered there, even though he suspected that there was a potential murderer among us. "If we're finished with our desserts, let's all assemble in the main area of the lodge."

A few folks clearly hadn't finished eating, though Jake and I had, but there were no complaints as the group left together.

As the guests started exiting, Cyn and Nan began to clear the tables. Evidently that wasn't in Hodge's plans, either. "Ladies, if you'll ask Choonie to join us, cleaning up will wait until later."

"What about Harley?" Cyn asked him. "Do you need him as well?"

"No, he's doing something else for me at the moment," Hodge said easily.

Jake and I made our way up to our host as the others filed out of the room. "What's going on, Hodge?" Jake asked him.

"Is London Peale really missing?" I asked in a rapid follow-up.

"If he is, we need to find him, and I mean right now," Jake insisted. "I don't know how he fits into what is happening here this weekend, but for all we know, he could be in serious trouble."

"Trust me, I'm doing everything that needs to be done at the moment. Just leave it up to me," Hodge said softly to us as he pulled us aside, away from the others.

Wow, George must not have told him *everything* about us. There was no way in the world that either one of us was going to allow him to stonewall us like that. "Hodge, we need to know what's going on right now, and I mean everything," Jake said.

The businessman looked startled by my husband's refusal to accept his answer as the final word, and I wondered when the last time was that someone had called him out on anything. It had clearly been a while.

It was a showdown, but there was little doubt in my mind who was going to win.

Every last dime of my money was on Jake.

"I can assure you both that London is fine," Hodge said, clearly irritated with Jake for pushing him. "Is that good enough for you, or must I produce the man to satisfy your curiosity? He's currently in his cabin sulking. I asked Harley to take him a plate of food, since he refused to join us for our meal. He's insisting on transportation off the island immediately, but it's going to have to wait until morning. I'm not risking the lives of my people just to satisfy his whims. Now, are you mollified by that?"

"I suppose we'll have to be," Jake said.

"Good. Then let's get on with the evening's main event." In a softer voice, he added, "Remember why you're both here."

"We're not about to forget," Jake said.

After Hodge left us and started for the front of the gathering space, I asked Jake softly, "Do you believe him?"

"Why do you ask? Don't you?" he asked in response.

"I'm not really sure at this point. Hodge is clearly not telling us something. I just don't know what it is."

"Do you mean about London Peale?"

"I'm talking about all of this," I said as I swept a hand around the folks now gathered near our host. "The only thing that is keeping me here besides the fact that there's only one boat off the island is that George is a friend of his."

"At least that's what Hodge told us," Jake answered.

"You don't believe him about that, either?"

"Does it even matter at the moment? I don't know about you, but I've never heard George mention the fact that he even knew anyone named Hodge Castor. We can't exactly call him and find out either, can we? As Cyn said, there's no cell phone service on the island, and I'm not sure how to go about finding the radio, let alone operating it. No, for now, we have to take Hodge at his word until we learn otherwise, but we need to keep a close eye on him, too."

My mind was swirling with conspiracy theories and rampant paranoia. If we couldn't trust our host, who could we put our faith in? That one turned out to be easy. I trusted my husband. End of statement.

Everyone else on the island was suspect.

"If you'll all gather over here," Hodge instructed us, staring straight at Jake and me, "we can get started."

I nodded, and as we moved forward, I whispered to Jake, "We'll finish this conversation later."

"You'd better believe we will," he said as we joined the other guests.

Hodge offered us all a tight smile before he started. "First, let me thank you all for coming to this extended weekend on the Star Island Retreat. Your reasons for being here are diverse, but we all desire the same outcome; to enjoy ourselves, and perhaps learn a little something about the world around us in the process. In the spirit of personal growth and friendly competition, I've planned a series of activities for each of you to participate in while you're here."

"Will you be joining us in the festivities?" Molly asked him.

Hodge frowned at being interrupted, and she immediately blushed from the negative attention. "No, I'm afraid not. I'll be in and out, and besides, it wouldn't be fair for me to take home the grand prize being offered to the winner."

"I thought this was supposed to be some kind of team-building exercise," Carl Wilson said.

"If you need to categorize it, think of it more like a competition," Hodge explained. "While it's true that there will be some team activities, there are also individual challenges as well. Ultimately, only one prize will be awarded, based on accumulated point totals throughout the weekend."

"So, what's the grand prize?" Christy Locke asked. "Does the winner get a share of stock in your company or something?"

"Ma'am, you of all people should know how reluctant I am

to part with those," he said with a smile that didn't hold a great deal of warmth in it.

Christy scowled a little at his response, but she didn't comment.

Hodge looked pleased about winning that particular exchange, and after a moment, he explained, "The ultimate winner will receive one of three prizes. It is entirely their choice, but once they've made their decision, I'm afraid that it's got to be final."

"So, what are our choices?" Barry Day asked, finally deigning to speak.

Hodge ticked off his fingers as he clarified his answer, "They are, in no particular order: twenty thousand dollars in cash; one hour with me to be spent in private conversation discussing any area of interest of the winner's choosing; or the deed to a specific parcel of land in Oakmont named River's Edge, which I've been told is of equal or greater value to the cash prize. I've held the land for nearly twenty years, and I can assure you, it's quite lovely."

"Who wouldn't take the money and run?" Christy asked.

"I'm going to opt for the hour of Hodge's time when I win," Barry Day answered, as though it were the only reasonable choice.

"*If* you win, you mean," Molly corrected him.

"Not if, but when," he answered smugly.

Hodge interrupted their banter. "Shall we begin? The first task is an individual one. Mrs. Bellacourt will hand out information sheets to each of you. There are seven items listed, all to be found here within the lodge. On each item, you'll find a code word or number of some sort. Return to me with all seven codes, no matter the order, and you win the first round."

"What if we want to team up on individual exercises?" I asked him.

"Then you will be disqualified for that event and receive zero points," Hodge said flatly.

That answered that.

I wasn't sure if I'd take the land or the money if I won. Then again, would Jake or I even receive the prize if we came out victorious, given the real reason we were there? What I was certain of was that the hour of Hodge's time would be worthless to me, though I knew that Barry Day, and perhaps Carl Wilson, would deem it to be the most valuable thing offered of all. What could they discuss with Hodge in an hour to make it worth twenty thousand dollars or a beautiful piece of land? I was fairly certain the knowledge they'd amass could be worth far more than the other choices, but I wouldn't even know the right questions to ask. I had a hunch that Molly and Christy would opt for the money, but then again, Christy's eyes had lit up at the mention of the land. Was there something there I didn't know about? Who was I kidding? I was in the dark about nearly everything when it came to this weekend. What had started off as being a fun, carefree getaway had turned into an instant pressure cooker.

Hodge let the prize announcement sink in, and then he stared straight at me as he added, "You are all eligible to win, no matter your current status, so use your time and resources wisely." He nodded to the staff. "Unfortunately, I'm afraid you all won't be able to participate. I'll need your services throughout the weekend, but since this is above and beyond what you each signed up for, you will all be rewarded in turn when the competition is over."

That got him a few smiles and nods from the staff, who were all doing their best not to look disappointed about being excluded from the festivities.

I was glad that Hodge had clarified his rules. Jake and I could take home the prize as readily as any of the other guests on hand. We wouldn't take a fee for helping Hodge find his would-be assassin, but this was something completely different.

"When I say begin, grab a sheet and get to work."

"Is there a time limit?" Molly asked.

"No, but if it takes the winner more than one hour to come forward with the correct answers, I'll be disappointed in every last one of you here, and most of you know how I hate to be let down." I saw Barry Day flinch a little at that. Had something gone on between them that had left the wunderkind coming up short in his employer's eyes? I wondered.

"When I say the word, you may begin."

We all waited with varying degrees of impatience, and after a delayed pause, Hodge simply said, "You may begin."

Barry Day and Molly Rider lunged for sheets immediately, while Jake and I lingered until there were only two papers left. It had been a fascinating experience standing back and observing the others, but we needed to get busy hunting ourselves. After all, there was no reason Jake and I shouldn't try to win as well, as long as it didn't interfere with our sleuthing. In a way, it was the perfect cover, throwing us into the mix with everyone else. Then again, winning for the sake of winning would be nice, too.

I took a sheet, and Jake grabbed his.

I read the list to myself, marveling at how much trouble Hodge—or more likely, Mrs. Bellacourt—had gone to.

There were seven cryptic lines printed out on the otherwise stark-white paper.

A clock without hands
On a team of nine
A different kind of pain
An ended discussion
A musical cord
A wordless tome
A jumbled tile

I saw a few of the guests still frowning at the list as I jumped into action. For a moment, I forgot why I was there. I loved games and puzzles, and now I'd been thrown into the middle of one, with prizes on the other end. Studying the room quickly, I started perusing the shelves and immediately found a few of the answers. A digital clock, one without hands, had the word *Blue* taped beneath it, so I jotted that down on my sheet next to the clue.

I should have been a little more circumspect, because the moment I put it down, Molly Rider pounced on it and read the word as well.

"Hey, that's no fair," I said.

"The rest of us deserve to read the clue, too," she said with a smile.

When I refused to budge any further, Molly started following the others around when a whistle sounded. Evidently she'd found what she believed was a winning strategy, and she was sticking to it.

Hodge kept staring at his distant relative for a few moments before he spoke. "Molly, that's a direct violation of the ethical code. Any clue found by a guest will be off limits to the rest of you for five minutes."

"But you didn't tell us that at the start," Molly protested.

"Sorry about that," our host said, though his grin showed that he felt no remorse whatsoever. "My game, my rules. You may wait in the dining room until you are released." He then turned to Cyn. "Start the clock. Let her come back in five minutes."

"Yes, sir," she said with a smile.

Molly was upset, but there was really nothing she could do but follow the rules, no matter how fluid they appeared to be.

"How are we supposed to know when five minutes are up for each clue?" Carl Wilson asked truculently.

"That's what Nan is doing. She'll announce when each clue is free again, but only one of you can use it until the time limit kicks in again."

That complicated things, but in a way, it also played into my strong suit. I'd always been good at puzzles and games, and so was Jake. I saw him grinning as he turned over an empty water pitcher on a side table, and I noted that Nan wrote it down. Jake had found a clue of his own.

I decided to head to the shelves that held games, books, and other diversions, and started looking through them.

It turned out to be a good decision.

In quick order, I found: *the jumbled tile*, which featured a clue printed beneath the Scrabble board game; *the wordless tome*, a dusty old diary that was blank throughout but for the key word printed on the last page; and *a musical cord*, which happened to go along with an old-fashioned radio buried in back. I was on a roll, finding four of the answers quickly, but I waited to write my new answers down until I'd finished searching that part of the room. Jotting down, *Green, Yellow, Purple,* and *Red*, if anyone was watching me, they'd have no idea where I'd found anything, since I'd also picked up a few random objects along the way and smiled, so that if anyone was shadowing me, they might be thrown off by the red herrings. I went over the rest of the list and pondered the clues Hodge had given us. I realized that it must nearly be time for Jake's pitcher to be free, but only Christy was watching it. I moved randomly until I got near it, and I started staring at Nan instead of the pitcher as I waited for the final seconds to pass.

Just as she was about to speak, I grabbed the pitcher, only to hear the whistle blow. When I looked up, Hodge was frowning at me.

"She was about to release it," I protested quickly before he could speak. "The time limit is what matters, not the announcement."

Hodge looked at Nan, and she quickly confessed, "The time really was up. I just hadn't publicized it yet."

"You may continue, then," Hodge said with a grin.

"That's not fair," Christy protested.

"Sorry, but any questions or disputes must be taken up with the rules committee," Hodge said, laughing. "You get three guesses who runs the rules committee."

The pitcher, or something *on a team of nine*, a baseball team, had the word *Gray* written on it. All I had left were *the different pain*, and *the ended discussion*. I kept walking around the room, trying to figure out what the clues could mean, when I saw Jake drop his pencil. No one else paid any attention to him, but I kept watching him as he glanced under the nearby table. That's when I got it! *The ended discussion* was one that was tabled! How clever of my husband! I pretended not to notice as a few other shouts surrounded me. Molly was back in the game, and this time she was turning things over with a vengeance, intent on making up for lost time. I'd save the table until the time limit was up, and in the meantime, I'd started looking for the *different kind of pain*. What could that mean? I hated thinking of anyone being in pain, especially since I didn't understand the clue. I happened to glance out the window as I walked past it, and there, partially hidden by a heavy curtain, was the word *Turquoise* taped to the glass. Pane. Window pane. How obvious it was after I'd seen the clue. I wrote the word down and headed for Jake's table.

A quick glance under it showed the word *Tangerine*, and I had the first victory.

Before I could announce it though, the whistle blew. Hodge looked at Nan. "Is the table clue free yet?"

She looked saddened to admit, "No, not for ten more seconds."

I'd forgotten all about the time limit in my excitement!

"Sorry, Suzanne. Into the dining room you go."

"But I have the solution," I protested.

"Good for you, but I'm afraid your competitors have five minutes to best you."

I reluctantly went into the dining room, amazed that I'd missed winning by a mere ten seconds. Cyn was sympathetic as well. "Sorry about that. Who knows? Maybe you'll still win."

"I have a hunch some of the others were nearly as close as I was," I said with a shrug. "I'm just sorry you don't get to play."

"Oh, we're playing a game of our own with Hodge at the moment," she said.

"Do tell," I encouraged her.

"I really shouldn't," she answered.

"Come on, live up to that name of yours and sin a little," I replied with a smile, trying to cajole her into telling me.

"I really can't," she said as she glanced around the room. We were obviously alone, but she was just as clearly reluctant to talk to me about whatever secret she was holding. It made me think yet again that we were being watched by someone, though as far as I knew, everyone on the island was either playing the game or aiding the host.

With one obvious exception.

Could London Peale's absence have been contrived to allow him to spy on us all for his former friend? Perhaps they'd reconciled, and Hodge had enlisted his aid this weekend. I didn't know what to think, but I did realize that any conversations I had with my husband from now on would take place outside, and hopefully out of the range of any hidden microphones.

When I felt that five minutes had surely passed, I asked Cyn, "Is it time yet?"

"You have precisely two minutes and ten seconds left. Sorry."

"That's okay," I said, when I was surprised to see the dining room door open. Who else had just violated one of Hodge's rules?

CHAPTER 7

"FUNNY, BUT I NEVER THOUGHT of you as a rule breaker," I said to Carl Wilson as he entered the dining area.

"I didn't realize anyone had found my clue!" he protested. "Were you the one who found the musical cord?"

"I was," I admitted it.

"I didn't see you do it, though," he answered angrily. "I was looking all over the piano, but there was nothing there. Then I started thinking about other kinds of music, so I went in search of a radio. The second I found it, Hodge blew that confounded whistle of his and banished me to this room!"

"I'm sorry," I said.

"You should be," Wilson said. "I think that little snot Barry Day is about to win. If he gets this prize, he's well on his way to that hour with Hodge."

"Why is that so valuable to you both?" I asked, genuinely wanting to know.

"How could it not be? Hodge has built an empire from the ashes of several failures! His insights are priceless. I can think of three questions off the top of my head that could change the course of the rest of my life! The way I figure it, I have one last shot to go out in a blaze of glory, and if I can do it, I will. If nothing else, I'd love to thwart Barry Day one final time. I've got to win that prize!"

"Is your future really all that bleak if you don't win?" I asked him.

The attorney seemed to realize that he may have said too much. "What? No. I'm fine. All I'm asking is who wouldn't like the opportunity to improve their lot in life? Even a donutmaker could use some extra cash, or am I mistaken?"

"Don't get me wrong; I like dough as much as the next person," I said with a smile. Wilson didn't get the pun, which made me a little sad for him. "It's nothing I'm not used to living without, though."

"Well, good for you," he said with a frown. "I, on the other hand…"

Whatever he was about to say was drowned out by three short whistle blasts, accompanied by an air horn.

Unless I missed my guess, someone had just taken first place away from me.

Barry Day was smiling triumphantly as we walked back into the main hall, holding his sheet aloft as though it were a trophy. "I did it. Sorry you lost." I didn't even care that there was no sorrow in his voice at all. I'd mostly wanted to win for the sake of winning. The prize offerings were just a bonus, as far as I was concerned.

"I solved the puzzle first. I can live with that," I said.

"Well, doesn't that make you special?" He turned to his boss. "When do we get that talk? I'm ready right now if you are."

"Hold on, Barry. Congratulations on winning, but this is just one part of the contest. Tomorrow, there will be a scavenger hunt, and the day after that, we will hold the final competition."

The young man looked disappointed for a moment before asking, "If I win tomorrow, can we dispense with the third contest altogether?"

"In case that happens, yes, but I warn you, it's going to be getting more difficult as we continue."

"Bring it on," Barry said, his face flushed from his victory.

"The color choices were curious," I said. "Is there any significance to them?"

"No, I just thought it would be more interesting than numbers or simple letters."

"I thought they might spell out a code word or something," I said. "I tried to figure it out while I was in my timeout, but I didn't have any luck."

Hodge grinned at me. "Now that you mention it, that would have been a nice touch, but I'm afraid I simply didn't think of it. I like the way you process information, Suzanne."

Day wasn't all that pleased that I was stealing a bit of his thunder. "What's going to be involved in the scavenger hunt? Do you have any tips for us before we get started?"

Hodge wasn't about to let a clue slip out. "Not right now. The master sheet is locked in my safe upstairs, and copies won't be printed out until they are needed tomorrow. For now, you've all had a big day, so I suggest you retire to your cottages, and we'll meet back here bright and early tomorrow morning. Breakfast is at seven, and it's not optional. Anyone missing the meal won't be allowed to participate in the day's events. You all know my habit of going to bed early and rising before dawn, and for this long weekend, I expect you all to adhere to my schedule. Good night."

Our host left the large open space and was heading for his hidden elevator when Mrs. Bellacourt spoke. Reading from her clipboard, she said, "As a reminder to each of you, here are your cottage assignments. Mr. Wilson, you're in Star Bright. Mr. Day, you've got Star Shine. Ms. Locke, you're in Star Fire. Mr. Bishop, Mrs. Hart, you're in Star Light. Miss Rider, you're here in the lodge in Burst 2. Any questions?"

"How are we supposed to find our way out there in the dark?" Wilson complained.

"There are signposts out front leading to each of the cottages, and the paths are lit at night by solar lights. There should be no danger of getting lost along the way unless you choose to wander off the lit walkways. I strongly suggest that you do not. While there are no natural predators on the island, there are many hidden pitfalls that will be hard to see in the dark. Good night."

"Hang on," Molly Rider said. "Why am I the only one staying in the lodge?"

"I too am housed here, as well as Mr. Castor and the entire staff. I believe you'll find the accommodations more than adequate for your needs."

"Mr. Peale didn't show up for dinner *or* the puzzle search. Why does he get a cottage of his own?"

"You'll have to take that up with Mr. Castor," she said in a dismissive tone. "That is all. Have a pleasant night, and please be prompt tomorrow morning. Your cottages are supplied with alarm clocks, so if you believe you will be in any danger of oversleeping, I suggest you use them. Mr. Castor, as I shouldn't need to remind any of you, is very serious about punctuality."

There were several nods, but Jake and I had no knowledge of Hodge's preferences one way or another. We walked outside together, with the others trailing along behind us, with the exception of Molly, who was staying at the main lodge alone.

"I don't know what she's complaining about," Wilson said. "I'd rather be in the lodge than be stuck out in the boonies alone."

"I'm sure she'll happily trade you," Day replied, obviously trying to goad the man into anger. "You know how flexible old Hodge is about his wishes being honored." The sarcasm was thick in his voice as he said it.

"No thanks. I'm good," Carl Wilson said, barely hiding his contempt for his fellow employee. "I suppose this is me," the attorney said as he pointed to the path that led to Star Bright. Mrs. Bellacourt hadn't lied. The paved walkways were well lit, and they had been cleared of snow as well. Harley must have been busy while we'd been inside eating and playing games.

"And this is me," Barry Day said as he took off down the path to Star Shine. He glanced behind him a few times while he was still in our view. What was he afraid of, that someone might be following him? I had a hunch that his bravado was mostly false, based on his reaction to being alone.

Christy Locke watched him go, and then she caught us observing her as well. She smiled at us warmly before she asked, "It was an interesting night, wasn't it?"

"I saw you react when Hodge mentioned the land offering as a potential prize," I said. "Is the parcel significant to you?"

"No, not that I know of," she said, her words faltering a little as she spoke. Christy was obviously lying, but I didn't have any leverage to get her to tell me the truth, and she was clearly not interested in answering my question otherwise. "Good night to you both," she said, and then she was on her way as well.

As Christy headed down the path to Star Dust, Jake took my hand and we started toward Star Light together. Heading down the path, I took the opportunity to share my suspicions with him before we were in a place that was possibly bugged. "I have a feeling that we're under constant surveillance while we're here."

"You, too?" Jake asked me.

"You suspected it as well?"

"Suzanne, Hodge's timed entrance can't be explained any other way. I've been trying to find the opportunity to say something to you, but I haven't had a chance. I'm beginning to wonder if that was intentional as well. I can't help but feeling that Hodge is up to something more than just trying to find a potential assassin."

"You could be right. I know he bears watching. Then it's

agreed. If we need to talk, we do it outside. After all, he can't bug the entire island, can he?"

"I wouldn't put it past him, but we should be all right. After all, he wouldn't expect anyone to guess what he's up to. To be fair, we both might just be overreacting to the tenseness of this situation."

"True, but it's better to take precautions we don't need than to ignore our instincts at our own peril," I replied.

Jake grinned at me and squeezed my hand. "I couldn't have said it any better myself."

"That's high praise indeed." I released my hand from his and rubbed my arms. "Man, the temperature really drops quickly out here, doesn't it? I'm beginning to wish that I'd packed a warmer jacket. It will be nice getting inside. Hopefully there will be a nice roaring fire waiting for us in the cottage."

"I would expect nothing less, but I'm afraid we're not going to be able to enjoy it, at least not right away."

I had a feeling what my husband was planning from the moment he spoke. "Let me ask you something. If we're going to go to Star Gaze and make sure London Peale is okay, which is what I suspect your plan is, then why are we going to our cottage first?"

"I can't trust these pathway lights," Jake said as he looked around. "I brought a pair of powerful small flashlights with me, and they're in my luggage at the cottage."

"Why on earth did you bring those along? Did you have a hunch we'd be sleuthing before we even got here?" I asked him with a grin.

"No, but I suspected that we might have to endure at least one power outage during our visit, and I wanted to be prepared. I'm just sorry I didn't bring my sidearm with me."

I'd been the one who'd convinced him to come unarmed. I didn't have anything against guns in general, but I'd wanted a tranquil weekend without being reminded that my husband usually had to carry a weapon around for protection. It had been a foolish thing to insist on, but it was too late to do anything about it now. We'd just have to do the best we could with what we had and hope for the best. The history of my investigations was rife with ad-libbing, and I hoped that once again, we'd manage to come out on the right end of things when all was said and done.

We got to Star Light soon enough, and I tried the front door, not entirely happy to find that it hadn't been locked. At least there *was* a lock, and I sincerely hoped we found the key inside. Otherwise, I wouldn't be able to get a wink of sleep knowing that someone could just walk in on us unannounced.

The place looked as though it could be featured in a magazine shoot without a hint of further preparation. The walls were plastered and painted a faint shade of gray, while the wood ceiling of the open room had been stained a lovely shade of tan that matched the main lodge. Oversized furniture filled the space, and a rock fireplace held a happily dancing fire. The bed was off to one side, heaped high with quilts that all looked handcrafted, and there was a small bathroom just off to one side. There were no televisions in sight, but there was a fair supply of books and games in case boredom set in, which I had a feeling would not be happening on this trip. All in all, it looked like a lovely place to spend a few nights if we weren't there to help prevent a murder, at any rate. Our bags had been placed on stands, and Jake dove into his to grab the promised flashlights. I, on the other hand, took a heavier jacket from my bag than the one I'd worn to the island and grabbed a knitted hat as well.

"Are you ready to go?" Jake asked me.

"Nearly," I said as I scanned the room for some kind of

weapon I might be able to use. The best I could come up with happened to be a bit of a cliché, but a fireplace poker should still do nicely.

Jake grinned at me. "Smart."

"I know, it's old school, but it will work. Are you going unarmed?"

He scanned the room for a moment and finally settled on a hefty piece of firewood. "This should do the trick."

"Aren't we a couple of armed desperados," I said with a grin.

"I don't know. I wouldn't go up against us," my husband added happily. He seemed to be enjoying himself much more than he had when he thought we were just going away on a mini-vacation. It was clear that Jake was in his element, and I wondered how we could extend the spark in his eyes past this trip. He still hadn't found a way to fill his days, but I had a hunch that he'd soon be doing something again. His mind was just too active to retire at such an early age.

"Lead on," I said as I glanced once more around the cozy cottage before braving the cold again. The air outside seemed to have a harsher bite to it after enjoying the warmth of our comfy space for even a few minutes, and I hoped that we'd find London Peale safe and sound in the Star Gaze cottage, though I wouldn't have put any money on it.

Something was clearly amiss with Star Island.

I just wasn't sure what it was yet, but I had a hunch that Jake and I were about to find out.

CHAPTER 8

"**I**S THAT SOMEONE AHEAD ON the path coming our way?" I asked Jake as we neared the main lodge again. There was no way we could figure out how to go directly to Star Gaze from our cottage, so we needed to retrace our steps back to the central hub before we went off in search of London Peale.

"It is," Jake whispered as he pulled me off the path into the surrounding trees. The snow crunched a little under our feet as we dodged behind some spruce trees, and we made it just in time before the mysterious figure got close enough for us to make out.

It was Harley, which wasn't alarming in and of itself, but the ax in his hands was more than a little disturbing. Was he out chopping firewood on this dark evening, or were his intentions more nefarious than that?

"Should we do something?" I whispered to Jake.

My husband shook his head, and I noticed that he was still holding onto me tightly. Was he trying to keep me from stepping back out onto the path? There was no need to do that. Until we could determine what the young handyman was up to, I was more than willing to stay in the shadows.

After Harley passed us, I was about to step back out onto

the path when Jake tugged at my arm. "Hang on a second," he whispered in my ear. "Give him a little time to get ahead of us."

I did as he suggested, and boy, was I ever glad that I had. Four seconds later, Harley came back, looking perturbed about something. What did he have to scowl about? As he neared the lodge again, I was surprised to see him suddenly turn his head toward the woods, as though he'd just heard something that we hadn't been privy to. Bolting off the path, he headed straight into the dense copse of trees!

I was suddenly glad that we'd stayed right where we'd been hiding.

As we heard him crashing through the woods in the distance, Jake nodded and finally released my arm. "We should be okay now."

"Where was he going with that ax, and why did he veer off the path so suddenly?" I asked him.

"I don't know, but I'm about to find out," Jake said as he hurried after Harley.

It was my turn to grab my husband's arm. "Are you sure that's really wise?"

"What choice do we have? Something's clearly going on, and we need to see what it is. There's really nothing else we can do, is there?"

"Maybe not, but considering the fact that a chunk of wood and an iron poker don't present much of a challenge for a man with an ax, we don't stand much of a chance if there's a direct confrontation. Besides, we don't even know what he's up to. We came out here to check on London Peale, remember?"

"Suzanne, I know what you're saying makes perfect sense," Jake said, clearly a little irritated with me for using logic against him. "I just don't like the look of what we just witnessed."

"I'm not particularly happy about it, either, but if you ask me, we should go check on London Peale first. I've got a feeling Harley can take care of himself."

"If he's one of the good guys," Jake opined. "Which I'm still not entirely convinced of. Are you?"

Before I could reply, suddenly there was a loud and heavy grunt in the direction of where Harley had just vanished, as though someone had just had the breath knocked out of them, and all of my earlier reasoning went out the window.

"Someone's clearly in trouble," Jake said, and without waiting for me or my approval, he took off after Harley. "We can't just let it go now."

I had no choice but to follow him. Jake was right. If someone was in immediate danger, it was our duty to help them and leave the mystery of London Peale's absence for later. Whether Harley was in trouble himself or someone else was in jeopardy because of the caretaker/handyman, we needed to see if we could help.

I spotted the body in the snow before Jake did.

Hurrying toward it, my flashlight bobbing up and down as I ran, my husband caught up with me quickly enough, but I made it there first.

Harley was lying facedown in the snow, and what was worse, the ax was nowhere to be seen.

CHAPTER 9

"I S HE DEAD?" I ASKED Jake as I knelt down beside my husband, who was frantically checking the young man for any signs of life.

"No, I've got a pulse, and it's surprisingly strong and steady," Jake said, smiling up at me.

"What do you think happened here?"

"That's what I plan to find out," Jake replied. Shaking Harley's shoulder vigorously and then turning him over to face us, my husband asked the handyman loudly, "Harley? Can you hear me? Are you okay?"

I saw Harley's eyes flutter open as both his hands went to the back of his head. "Somebody clobbered me from behind. My head feels like it was cracked open like a walnut."

I felt around his hair. There was a growing knot there, but fortunately no blood. Whether the thickness of his hood or the hardness of his head had saved him, it appeared that Harley was going to be okay.

The handyman started to stand, and he managed it, though he stumbled a little as he did. Fortunately, Jake was there and ready to steady him.

"Should he be up and walking around so soon?" I asked.

"I don't believe too much damage was done. We need to get him up to the lodge," Jake said, "and I don't know about you, but I don't think we can carry him even with two of us."

"I'm fine," Harley said, brushing Jake's steadying hand away.

77

Instead of heading back to the lodge, though, the handyman started off in the opposite direction.

"Where are you going? The lodge is that way," I corrected him. "Are you sure you're okay? You might have a concussion. You must be turned around."

"I'm not going back to the lodge. Whoever clobbered me took off that way. They jumped me from behind and stole my ax. Do you think there's a chance I'm letting them get away with that?"

"Whoever did it is long gone," Jake said, trying to convince the young man to come with us.

"It doesn't matter. There are still tracks in the snow. Now, are you coming with me, or do I have to do this by myself?"

It was clear that he wasn't about to be dissuaded, so we honestly only had one choice. "We'll come with you," Jake agreed.

I glanced at my husband as I shined my light into my face to show him my displeasure with the idea, but he merely shrugged. I was certain that he would have wanted to do the exact same thing as Harley was insisting if the circumstances had been reversed, and I was in no mood to argue with either one of them at the moment. "Fine, but if you lose your balance, and I mean just once, we're heading straight back to the lodge."

There must have been something in my voice, because Harley stopped long enough to glance back in my direction and then at Jake. "Is she serious?"

"I'd do what she says if I were you," Jake replied.

"Fine. Come on."

Harley started off into the trees and the snow, using the faint amount of moonlight coming through the clouds to show him the way. I handed him my flashlight, which he took gratefully. I could see fine following the two of them. We started off at a fast pace, but it soon ended in a large copse of evergreen trees. There, the snow hadn't been able to penetrate as deeply, and footprints tended to blur into one another as the snow thinned. Then Jake frowned at the ground before taking his light and shining it on a nearby tree. I looked and saw that someone had taken Harley's ax and had cut away a bough, using it as a broom to obscure their footprints even more.

"Whoever did this was too smart for us," Jake said as he put a hand on Harley's shoulder.

"For now, maybe," the young man said reluctantly.

"Come on. Let's get you to the lodge."

Even Harley had to admit that following the trail had become almost impossible given the circumstances, so he turned on his heel and headed back, but not before facing the trees and bellowing, "You think you've won, but all you've done is made me mad. I'll find you, and when I do, you'll be eating that ax from the handle up."

I didn't know if it made him feel any better, but the woods around us were plunged into deathly silence as the three of us headed back to the lodge to make sure no more damage had been done to the young man than a knot on his head and a severely bruised ego.

It took us a few minutes to rouse Mrs. Bellacourt, and when she finally came to the door, it was clear that we'd woken her. How early must she go to sleep? Evidently she'd adopted her boss's habits completely, and it took her a moment to realize what we were telling her.

"I don't understand," she said. "Are you saying that someone attacked you, Harley?"

"Yes, ma'am," he said as he rubbed his head and winced a little from the pain. "They jumped me from behind, or they never would have managed it."

"Tell her the rest of it," Jake prodded.

"They got my ax, too," he admitted.

"On an island with no real weapons, I'm assuming an ax could be a very dangerous weapon indeed," Jake said. "We need to wake Hodge and tell him what's going on."

"Hold on one moment," Mrs. Bellacourt said, and then she accessed an intercom I hadn't noticed before. "Cynthia, Nanette, Harley is upstairs. He's been attacked."

"Coming," Cyn said hastily, and a few moments later, she and Nan were with us.

"Take him to the infirmary and see to his head, please," she instructed the young women.

As they headed back toward the kitchen, where the infirmary was located, Harley was telling his story yet again, this time to a rapt audience.

"I'm sure he'll be fine," Mrs. Bellacourt said after they were gone.

"I wish I could be as certain as you seem to be," I said. "He could easily be suffering from a concussion or even a cracked skull and not even know it. We need to get him medical attention, and I mean tonight."

"I'm afraid that's not possible," she said stiffly.

"What do you mean, it's not possible? Maybe not for you, but your boss isn't going to want a lawsuit on his hands if something happens to one of his employees," I said.

"Each staff member here signed a much more detailed waiver than you did," she replied. "Besides, when I say that it's impossible, that's exactly what I mean. Mr. Castor has left the island momentarily, taking the only boat with him in the process."

"Then call someone on the radio," Jake insisted.

"That's why Mr. Castor left. Apparently someone damaged the radio, so there is no communication available other than direct contact with the outside world."

"So, he left us all here trapped like rats on a sinking ship while he ran for safety," I said.

Mrs. Bellacourt looked thoroughly displeased by the analogy, but I didn't care. As far as I was concerned, that was exactly what he'd done by abandoning us on Star Island while he made his escape. "I can assure you, we are all perfectly safe here."

"Tell Harley that," Jake said. "And there's really no other way off the island?"

"Not until Mr. Castor returns," she said stiffly. "Now, if you'll excuse me, I need to go see about Harley."

"I thought you just said that he would be perfectly fine," I reminded her with a bite in my voice.

She didn't deign to answer; she simply disappeared into the kitchen where the infirmary was located.

"What do we do now?" I asked Jake once we were alone.

"Do we really have any choice? Nothing that's happened tonight should change our minds."

"We could always just head back to our cottage, bolt the door, and wait until morning comes when we can actually see what we're doing," I suggested.

Jake laughed softly. "Suzanne, you don't honestly think I'm going to choose that option, do you?"

"No, of course not, but a girl can hope, can't she?" I asked, knowing that there was no way my husband would be dissuaded once he came up with a plan of action.

"We need to collect our weapons and go check on London Peale. As a matter of fact, it might not be a bad idea to round everyone up and bring them back here to the lodge after we pay a visit to Star Gaze. That way we can keep an eye on all of our suspects at once."

"Boy, they're going to just love that, aren't they?" I asked, envisioning the reactions we'd most likely get from the other guests on the island.

"At this point, how they feel is the least of our worries. Let's go check on Peale first, and after that, we can worry about the others."

"I'm right behind you," I said.

We walked back out into the brisk night air, and I was glad that Jake had been thoughtful enough to pack those two flashlights. After finding our discarded weapons where we'd left them in the woods, we headed back to the path and finally started down the way to Star Gaze, the cottage London Peale supposedly was occupying. How long had it been since we'd started off on the task of checking in on him? Surely a few hours had passed in the interim. As I glanced at my watch, I was startled to see that only thirty minutes had gone by since we'd first set off from our own safe and snug cottage.

I had to admit that I felt a little better having that poker in my hand as we started down the path toward the missing guest's cottage. Jake seemed happier as well with the firewood chunk by his side, and I knew that it could be a fine weapon if that was required.

I hoped and prayed that he wouldn't need it, though.

As we approached the cottage, I saw that the lights were mostly out inside. Had London Peale gone off to bed, or was there another, more dire reason the place was cloaked in darkness?

One way or the other, we'd find out soon enough.

CHAPTER 10

J AKE DIDN'T EVEN HAVE TO flip the light on once we were
inside. The cottage was, as I'd expected, unlocked, but what
we hadn't been able to see clearly from the outside was that
the bathroom light was on, giving us enough illumination to see,
if not everything, then certainly enough. The door was open just
a crack, but it still offered enough illumination for us to make
out the barest outlines of the space.

My husband turned to me as he flipped off his flashlight and
held a finger to his lips, asking for silence. He didn't have to
ask me twice. The cottage was laid out much like ours was, but
instead of being warm and toasty inside, it was quite cold. Jake
pointed to his chest and then to the bathroom. After a moment,
he gestured toward me and pointed to my feet.

I shook my head rather violently. It was clear that he was
asking me to stay right where I was while he investigated, but it
should have been more than obvious to him that I wasn't about
to do as he suggested.

After a moment, he shrugged, and then we set off for the
bathroom door together.

It was nearly closed, but there was enough of a wedge of
light coming through to show that one mighty push would be
enough to fling it open. Jake glanced back at me for a second,
and I held my poker in the air, ready to back his play if he
needed to jump into action.

Heaving the door with a resounding thud, I looked inside to see that Hodge hadn't left the island after all.

Instead, he was standing over a stranger's body, holding an ax that was now decidedly quite a bit bloodier than it had been when I'd last spied it.

"You killed him," I said, finding it hard to grasp the words.

"What? Of course I didn't. I just came in here and found him like this two seconds ago."

"It that's the truth, then why do you have an ax in your hands?" Jake asked him, gripping his own piece of firewood firmly as he spoke. To my husband's everlasting credit, he moved sideways and back toward where I was standing, and I wasn't even certain that he was aware of the fact that he was putting himself squarely between me and a possible murderer.

"What? No, it's not like that," Hodge said as he appeared to notice the ax in his hands for the first time. Dropping it to the floor, he protested, "I found it outside in the main room when I came to check on London. It worried me that he might be in trouble, and I didn't have a weapon at my disposal, so I picked the ax up. I couldn't even see the blood on it from out there. Anyone would have done the exact same thing in my place."

I wasn't entirely sure that he was right, but this was no time to debate the issue. "Mrs. Bellacourt told us that you'd taken the boat and left Star Island," I said in an accusatory tone.

"That's because that's what I wanted her to believe," Hodge said as Jake knelt down by the man's prone body and touched his skin. I stepped forward, just in case Hodge went for the ax again. Jake wasn't the only one who could get his spouse's back. If our host made one false step toward the weapon, he'd be eating the poker in my hands. "Is he…"

"Unless I miss my guess, he's been dead at least half an hour, if his body temperature is any clue," Jake said matter-of-factly.

"It's awfully cold in here," I said, shivering from more than just the chilled air. "Could the killer have left the outside door open to cool the body in order to throw off a reasonable guess at the time of death?"

"The front door *was* wide open when I got here a few minutes ago," Hodge acknowledged.

"Why were you just standing there over your friend's body when we came in?" I asked him.

Our host looked embarrassed as he admitted, "I suppose I just froze. Seeing him like that seemed to make my entire body and mind shut down."

"I presume that was the late London Peale," I said.

"Yes, it's him all right. Where exactly was he struck with the ax?"

Jake examined the body briefly. "It appears that someone drove that ax into his back, and then they immediately pulled it out again." He glanced up at Hodge as he added, "If you're going to be sick, do it outside."

"No, I'm all right," he said, and then he glanced in my direction. "Suzanne, why aren't you screaming or something?"

"Why, because I'm a weak little woman?" I asked him. "Sadly, this isn't the first dead body I've ever seen, though I keep hoping that the next one will be the last."

"There's nothing we can do for him now," Jake said as he stood. He looked around and then grabbed one of the heavy towels from the rack, and I thought he was going to place it over the man's head. Instead, my husband gently wrapped up the ax with it and moved it to one side.

"My prints are going to be all over that," Hodge protested.

"You'd just better pray that someone else's are as well," Jake replied as I grabbed another towel and gently placed it over the man's body. It was one of those giant sheet towels, and it mostly managed to cover the late London Peale.

"What I don't get is who would want to kill London?" Hodge asked as he slumped down in one corner of the room. "It just doesn't make sense."

"Who else did he know here besides you?" I asked him.

"No one else, or so I thought," Hodge said. "What are we going to do? We can't leave the island, and we can't communicate with the outside world, either."

"You were about to tell us about the boat," I suggested.

"Somebody put a hole in it big enough to push a volleyball through," he said with disgust. "I got restless and took a walk around the grounds, as I often do at night when I'm here. I happened to check the boat, and it was just sinking out of sight when I got to it. There's no way we can retrieve it, but even if we could, we can't patch it. That engine is bound to be ruined too, and the oars were all smashed to pieces when I got there."

"Mrs. Bellacourt said that the radio was ruined. Was that true?"

He nodded angrily. "Somebody wrecked it beyond repair. Whoever did it didn't want anyone coming to our rescue."

"Surely you have a contingency plan," I said. "I can't imagine a man of your wealth and imagination having no backup strategy in place."

"I thought the boat and the radio would be enough. I won't make that mistake again, but there's nothing we can do about it now."

"So what's our plan? Do we just wait around for someone to notice that we haven't left the island and come looking for us?" I asked him.

"We won't have to wait that long. I've got a cleanup crew coming here in two days to help shut everything down for the season. If we can hold out for thirty-six hours, we should be okay."

"That's a lot to ask, given the current circumstances," I said.

Hodge turned to Jake. "You were an investigator for the state police. Surely you wouldn't come on a vacation unarmed."

"If that were true, would I have come in holding a piece of firewood just now?" Jake asked. As he did, I noticed he took one step closer to the ax, which might very well be the only viable weapon on the island, even if it had already been used to kill one of the guests.

"Don't blame him; it was all my fault," I said. "I asked him not to bring it."

"It doesn't matter at this point," Jake said dismissively. "The killer didn't need an exotic weapon to dispatch this man. A simple ax appeared to do the job nicely."

"At least we still have power on the island," I said.

"That's from our generator," Hodge said proudly. "Give me a little credit. I wasn't about to leave our power supply to chance. We could get underground cables from the mainland to the lodge, but it would have been prohibitively expensive. The generator is a much better choice."

At that moment, we were all plunged into darkness.

Evidently whoever was pulling the strings on Star Island had decided that we'd all be better suited to quite literally stumbling around in the darkness.

CHAPTER 11

"SERIOUSLY? DID WE JUST LOSE power, too?" I asked. Hodge frowned as Jake shined a light into his face. "Put that somewhere else, would you?" our host complained. "It might just need refueling. That was one of Harley's jobs, and I know for a fact that he was supposed to do it tonight."

"He was probably kind of busy at the time getting conked on the head and having the murder weapon taken from him," I said.

"What? What happened to him? Is he dead, too?" Hodge asked, clearly concerned about his young employee. As a matter of fact, he was showing more remorse about Harley than he was his late friend, quite dead and lying on the floor, mostly being covered by a bath towel.

"No, chances are he's going to be fine, but he's going to at least have a nasty bump on his head in the morning," Jake said. "I don't like this one bit."

"Which part is that, the fact that one of my oldest friends has just been murdered, that we're stranded on an island without any hope of rescue, or that our power supply has been shut down?"

"Take your pick," Jake said.

"We need to get everyone together at the lodge," Hodge said as he headed for the door. "Even if the power supply is completely down, there are solar panels on the roof, so we'll have LED lights, and the massive fireplace will keep us all from freezing to death while we figure this out."

Jake leaned down and picked up the ax. "I'm sorry. Were you under the impression that you were still in charge around here, Hodge?"

The man looked clearly startled by my husband's question. "Are you kidding? In case you've forgotten, this is my island, including everything on it."

"I understand that, but as far as I can determine at this point, there's a very good chance that you may be a murderer."

"That's absurd," he said, eyeing the covered ax in Jake's hands.

"Is it really, though?" I asked. "By your own testimony, you and the murder victim were having a great deal of trouble. Don't forget, we found you standing over the body holding what will undoubtedly turn out to be the murder weapon, and what's more, you contrived to give yourself an alibi before you came down here by telling Mrs. Bellacourt that you were going for help, thus justifying your absence to everyone else."

"It wasn't like that," Hodge explained, and then he looked oddly at me. "Why are we even having this conversation? I don't have to explain anything to you, young lady. After all, you're just a donutmaker."

I was about to rebut when Jake did it for me. "You'd better be careful about choosing your next words. Suzanne is one of the best investigators I've ever known, both professional and amateur, so I wouldn't underestimate her if I were you. Besides, everything she said was true, and while I may not be on active duty with the state police, I have official reserve status for as long as I live."

I had no idea if that were true or not, but it certainly sounded official. Hodge must have bought it too, given the circumstances. "Fine. I give up. Arrest me. What are you going to do, confine me to my room? Need I remind you that I'm the one who controls everything around here, whether you like it or not? Besides, if there's no power, there's no way to get into my suite upstairs."

"You need to be reasonable and look at things from our point of view. If you were in our shoes, what would you think?" Jake asked.

Hodge frowned for a moment before he spoke again. "I grant you that it looks bad for me, but I give you my word that I didn't kill London Peale. The real question is, is that enough?"

"How about sabotaging the radio or the boat? Will you give us your word on that as well?" I asked him.

"Don't be ridiculous. Why would I destroy my own possessions?"

"To make it look possible that someone else might have killed London Peale," Jake said.

I nodded my approval of my husband's comment, but Hodge clearly wasn't happy with the turn things had taken. "Fine. I can't convince you that I'm innocent, even though I am, and you can't lock me up without restricting your own access to every asset we have left on the island, not even considering the fact that we're without power. We're at a standoff, aren't we?"

"If it were me, I'd lock him up and worry about the rest of it later," I told Jake.

"You're awfully cold for a confectioner, aren't you?" Hodge asked.

"I'm a donutmaker. A confectioner does something completely different," I replied. "Where can we lock him up that we can be sure he stays?"

Jake frowned. "I have no idea."

"Trust me. Your best bet is to take me at my word that I'm innocent and let me help you find the real killer," Hodge said persuasively.

"What do you think, Suzanne?"

"I don't know," I said. "I'm going to have to rely on your

professional opinion on this one. I'm not afraid to admit that I'm in way over my head."

Jake mulled it over for at least ten seconds before he spoke again. "Hodge, while it's true that we need you, it doesn't necessarily mean that we have to trust you. You're to stay within my sight range, or my wife's, at all times, until this is over. Do you understand?"

"Why would I bring you here to find my possible killer if I were just going to murder someone else myself?" Hodge asked us. "It doesn't make sense. Let's at least try to be reasonable."

"You don't want us to do that," I said. "I can think of an obvious scenario where you discovered that London Peale was the one who tried to kill you, but you didn't find out until after you'd asked us here. You decided to take matters into your own hands, and after making up a pretext that you were leaving the island, you stalked Harley, hit him on the head, stole his ax, and while we were tending to him, you slipped down here and dispatched your onetime friend before he could finish what he started. You would have gotten away with it, too, if Mrs. Bellacourt hadn't dismissed us out of hand, freeing us to come here and find you clutching the murder weapon as you stood over the body."

"You sound so convincing that *I'm* not even sure I didn't do it, and I *know* that I'm innocent," he said reluctantly. "Go on, then. If you feel that strongly, lock me up."

"As much as that prospect appeals to me, I stand by my earlier suggestion," Jake said. "You need to stay close, but as far as anyone else is concerned, we go on, business as usual, until someone gets here to rescue us and take this off our hands."

It was my turn to be shocked. "Jake, are you actually suggesting that we don't tell anyone about the murder? We can't exactly go about our business and forget it even happened."

"As a matter of fact, that's exactly what we should do." He turned to Hodge. "Is there a key for this cottage, by any chance?"

"It's hanging by the door," Hodge admitted. "Why, what do you propose?"

"I think we should lock this door and tell everyone that London Peale has left the island. While we wait for your supply boat, we continue with your little games and try to figure out who the real killer is before reinforcements arrive." Jake hesitated, and then he glanced at me. "What do you think of it as a plan?"

"I'm not entirely sure we have any choice," I said. As screwy as his idea was—and it was odd enough to fit into Grace's and my realm of possibility—it was probably the best we could do, given the circumstances.

"Hodge? What do you think?"

"It makes sense to me," he replied. "If we can't get the generator restarted, we'll all still need to stay in the lodge tonight."

"Maybe we should do that anyway," I suggested.

"Why is that?" Jake asked.

"At least then we'd be able to keep tabs on everyone if we're all sleeping in the same room."

"Perhaps if one of us stays awake the entire night," Jake amended.

"We can split the shifts in two," I said.

"I can take a turn as well," Hodge offered, but then he must have seen the looks on our faces. "Never mind. Forget I said anything."

"So, it's a plan, then," Jake said.

"I'm not crazy about it either," I answered, "but it's better than anything I've been able to come up with myself."

Locking Star Gaze behind us, we made our way back to the main lodge, with me in front, Hodge next, and Jake taking up the rear. I was comforted knowing that my husband had the ax with him, but it still made me uneasy thinking that the man who'd brought us here to solve his own attempted murder might have taken matters into his hands and finished off his would-be killer himself.

CHAPTER 12

"WILL YOU LOOK AT THAT?" Jake said as he pointed to the lodge just ahead of us. Evidently the power outage had been temporary after all. Harley must have resupplied the generator. What did that do to our plans, though?

"Are we still going to gather everyone together at the lodge now?" I asked Jake.

He frowned as he hesitated under one of the lights shining down on us anew. "I don't see how we can do that now. What possible excuse could we use?"

"Besides the fact that London has been murdered, you mean?" Hodge asked.

"We decided to keep that to ourselves for now, and I don't see how having power again has changed anything," Jake reminded him.

"I don't think we have much choice," I said. "Unless we want to alarm everyone, we need to leave them where they are."

"What happens if the killer strikes again in the middle of the night, though?" Hodge asked us seriously. "Are we all going to feel as though we were somehow culpable by not telling my guests that there was a murderer among us?"

"I don't believe London Peale's death was random for one second, do you?" Jake asked him pointedly.

"At this point, I honestly have no idea *why* he was murdered.

For all I know, we could have a sociopath amongst us, picking us off one by one," he said eerily.

Jake frowned, and then he asked, "Do you keep the surveillance video you record, or are the files wiped every night?"

Hodge protested, but just a split second too late to make it feel earnest. "Security tapes? What are you talking about?"

"Don't bother denying it. We know the lodge is bugged," I said, though in fact we only just suspected it. "What we need to know is if there is video as well? And does it just cover the main lodge, or are the cottages being watched as well?"

Hodge wanted to bluff it out, but his friend's death must have shaken him more than he'd let on so far. He made one more feeble attempt at denial, though. "I don't know what you're talking about. That's nonsense."

"It's not, and we all know it," Jake said. "I'm sure the authorities will have something to say about you taping your guests covertly once they learn about it."

"It's not all *that* covert," Hodge said. "Do you remember the waivers you signed before you even took one step onto the island?"

"Of course we do," Jake said. "I'm absolutely positive that there was nothing about being videoed while we were here."

"That's where you're wrong," Hodge said, smiling slightly at his own cleverness. "It's well buried in the addendums of the document, but the consent is there. Do you honestly think I wouldn't take that basic precaution?"

"Then that means that you have video of the murder itself," my husband said solemnly.

"I wish. No, the system's been on the fritz for the past few days. The audio works in the lodge's main spaces, but the video has been down, and everything recording in the cottages has been on the fritz as well."

"Who exactly is aware of that?" I asked him.

"Do you mean about its existence, or the fact that it hasn't been working? Before tonight, I would have said no one, but you two certainly twigged onto it quickly enough. I'm curious. What gave me away?"

"It was the speed with which you joined us after I suggested we conduct a manhunt for London Peale. Why didn't you want that to take place?"

Hodge frowned. "The man was just stewing in his cottage. I knew perfectly well that he was fine. I'd hoped that, given a little time, he'd come around. Alas, he wasn't afforded that opportunity."

"So, you're saying that you have no idea who might have killed him."

"I honestly don't have a clue. Will you two be heading back to your cottage now that the lights are back on?"

"That's not happening," Jake told him. "You're not leaving our sight until we're off this island."

"Is that to protect me or to look out for the people around me?" he asked.

"Does it matter? I know there are enough couches for both of us in your penthouse. Suzanne and I will take turns keeping watch, and in the morning, we'll see if we can get to the bottom of this. Do you have any objections to that plan?"

"Would it matter even if I did?" our host asked us with a hint of sad laughter in his voice.

Jake just shrugged.

"If you put it that way, I suppose it doesn't. Why don't you go ahead and lead the way," I suggested.

We entered the lodge to find Mrs. Bellacourt standing near the elevator. She looked surprised to see her employer. "You're back, sir. Were you able to get a spare radio?"

"I'm afraid we're all going to be without any communication

gear until further notice, but let's keep that to ourselves, shall we?" Hodge asked.

"Of course, sir."

"How is young Harley doing?" he asked her. "Suzanne and Jake were kind enough to bring me up to speed on what's been going on."

"He's lapping up all of the attention from Cyn and Nan at the moment while Choonie is fixing him something to eat," Mrs. Bellacourt said with a hint of disapproval in her voice. "I have a feeling that he's not in nearly as much pain as he claims to be."

"Leave him be. He's earned it," Hodge said.

Mrs. Bellacourt turned to us. "I'm surprised to see you two here as well. I thought you had both gone off to bed."

"They were about to, but I've asked them to spend some time upstairs with me, instead," Hodge said, making it sound as though it had been his idea all along. "I see the generator is back in working order."

"Harley performed some kind of magic on it," the assistant said. "I suspect he forgot to switch over to the new tank."

"Well, as long as we have power again, it hardly matters. Now, if you'll excuse us, it's been a long day."

"May I get you anything before you retire, sir?" she asked him solicitously.

"No, I'm fine. Good night, Belle."

"Good night, sir." Almost as an afterthought, she turned and nodded to us as well as the three of us got on the hidden elevator and made our way to the penthouse. Was that a look of disapproval on her face, or was it more one of envy? Either way, it appeared that my husband and I were not Mrs. Bellacourt's favorite guests at the moment.

I'd have to somehow find a way to live with the disappointment.

Once we were upstairs, Hodge pointed to two smaller doors that I'd missed on our previous visit. "There are two guest rooms, so take your pick."

"Thanks, but we'll be staying out here," Jake said, feeling the couch cushion. "It's soft enough, so it will be fine."

"Suit yourself," Hodge said as he headed for his own bedroom.

"Hang on a second. We'd like to see those dossiers before you go to bed," I said.

"What? I thought we'd already covered that," Hodge said after frowning at me slightly.

"That was then; this is now. The game has changed," I said.

Jake nodded. "Get the files, Hodge, unless they're on your computer."

"No, I wouldn't trust them to the cyberworld," he said. After reaching into a desk drawer, he pulled out a thick pile of folders. "I can tell you right now this is a complete and utter waste of time. There's nothing in these that will help you figure out who killed London."

"Why don't you let us be the judge of that?" Jake said.

"Fine. Suit yourself." Hodge went into his bedroom and started to close the door.

I called out, "Leave that open, if you wouldn't mind."

"As a matter of fact, I do," our host protested. "What possible good will it do you to watch me as I sleep?"

"How do we know there aren't any secret passageways hidden in there?" Jake asked him.

"I suppose it's out of the question for you to take me at my word that there are not, given the circumstances."

Jake shrugged. I thought for a moment that Hodge would protest further, but he simply frowned and got into bed, not bothering to change before he did.

"Do you want the first shift, or should I take it?" Jake asked me as he tapped the folders with his fingers.

"I'm not sure that I can sleep at all, given what's happened," I said.

"I know what you mean. Let's divide these up, and then we can compare notes." He split the files in half. Jake got Barry Day's, Christy Locke's, and Carl Wilson's, while I got Molly Rider's, London Peale's, and one simply marked Staff. Jake smiled as he handed me a portion. "If you find anything interesting, let me know."

"Right back at you," I said as I picked up the first folder and started to read. Besides the pertinent data of age, birthplace, occupation, work history, and a full photograph, I noticed a series of notes about each person written by hand. I read Hodge's additions with interest, as I thought they might prove to be the most valuable bits of information of all.

Molly Rider: She honestly thinks that being related to me is some sort of golden ticket for her, which I've assured her repeatedly, it is not. Molly let slip once that she expects to inherit something, so she's a likely candidate for being my would-be assassin, though I've done my best to let her know that if anything happens to me, she's out of the will entirely. She seemed shocked when I told her, so maybe she took those three shots at me after all. Is she a viable threat? I couldn't say. I made one mistake with her, and the rest of them as well. Carl Wilson is changing my will, and in a fit of anger over being shot at, I let slip that we'll be making the changes at the end of the weekend. Not the brightest move on my part, I know that, but I was angry, and I'm afraid the others overheard it, too. Blast and blast.

So, Hodge had neglected to tell us about that! What, did he not think it was critical to our investigation or to our weekend stranded with several people who each had more than enough reason to want to see him dead?

"Jake, listen to this." I read the same passage softly to my husband, not wanting to wake Hodge, who was happily snoring away in the other room.

"For a supposed genius, the man's a bloody fool, isn't he?" Jake asked in disgust.

"It might explain the situation if we'd found *him* dead, but it doesn't make any sense that it was London instead."

"Does it say anything about any ties Molly might have had with the victim?" Jake asked.

"No, there's nothing here about that," I said as I leafed through the pages again. "I'm afraid we're going to have to ask that question ourselves."

"Listen to what I found," Jake said. "It says here in Barry Day's files that he's been trying to oppose the liquidation since he first heard about it. Evidently there's a board of directors for Hodge's main corporation, and Barry's been working behind his boss's back to get them to unseat him."

"Can they do that?" I asked. "I thought Hodge owned the majority of everything outright."

"Apparently he's been forced to sell off a few shares here and there over the years, and if Barry can get Christy Locke to vote her shares for his side, he might be able to stage a coup. He needs more time, though, and according to this, Hodge thinks he can win a battle in the boardroom, if it comes to that."

"That might explain Hodge's attempted murder, but why London's?"

"I don't know," Jake said as he looked through the other files. "Peale's file must be in your stack."

I looked and found it, and after cracking it open, I read the comments section aloud after glancing at the photo.

"London has been a problem for me for the past several months. I gave him his shares with my heartfelt thanks a long time ago. I never dreamed that generosity might bite me in the rump later. Like they say, no good deed goes unpunished. I tried to buy the

shares back recently, but London told me that he had a better offer from someone else, and it didn't involve money. The fool needs to be brought back into the fold, and I'll manage it, or one of us will die from the effort."

"That doesn't sound good," Jake said.

"Hodge clearly wrote that entry before the murder," I replied as I looked in on the sleeping man.

"Maybe so, but it shows that he had a motive for murder, if he was the one who killed his former friend."

"Why, to keep him from selling off his shares to another bidder? What makes Hodge think he can get London's heir to sell them to him, if the man himself wouldn't do it?"

"Maybe because *I'm* the one who will inherit them, now that London is dead," Hodge said from the doorway.

I hadn't even realized that he was awake.

How much had he heard, and had we said anything we wouldn't have wanted him to hear?

CHAPTER 13

"I FREELY ADMIT THAT I MADE a mistake with London giving him those shares, but the man saved my life once. How *else* could I repay him?"

"Do you mean that literally?" I asked him.

Hodge waved a hand through the air. "I won't discuss it, not now, not ever, and certainly not with you. Suffice it to say that I had my reasons. At least I was smart enough to add one rider to the gift. He could sell the shares to whomever he pleased, but no one else could inherit them but me, unless he had a child of his own. That wasn't going to happen, and I figured that London wasn't going to give up control over me by getting rid of his stocks, either. It seemed a safe enough bet at the time. Maybe I was wrong about that, but that's what I thought before this weekend." He gestured to the other files on the floor. "Have you found anything salacious there?"

"Not yet," Jake said. "Why, is there something we've missed?"

"That's not the point. I thought I was writing my private thoughts on who might want to kill me, not London Peale, and besides, they weren't meant for anyone else to see," he said with a heavy frown.

"You know, there's something that hadn't occurred to me until just now, seeing you standing there outlined in the shadows," I said.

"What's that?" Hodge asked me.

"Based on the photograph in his file, it's clear to me that

you and London Peale shared a rather remarkable build," I said. "Standing there like that backlit and all, your physical presence is much more like London's must have been than I realized when he was just lying there on the floor. It's hard to get a true sense of someone's height when they're prone."

"I hardly think that matters. After all, Carl Wilson has the same build as we both did, and nobody's murdered him, at least not yet."

Jake frowned. "He's also a good foot shorter than the two of you. Surely you've realized before now how similar your builds were."

"Yes, we commented on it on more than one occasion," Hodge said. He walked forward a few steps and then slumped down into a chair. "So that's what happened. Someone thought they were hitting me in the back with an ax, and they got poor London instead."

"It's a possibility," I said.

"Truthfully, now that you mention it, it's the only thing that makes sense," Hodge admitted.

"Well, it's not the *only* thing, but it's something we need to keep in mind as we move forward with the investigation," I said. Could it have really been as simple as a case of mistaken identity? We had to consider it a possibility, especially since London had been struck in the back, and not where the killer could see his face. Most likely the cottage had been dark, quite a bit darker than the penthouse was at the moment. I hadn't been able to see Hodge's features in the shadows as he'd stood there, and he'd been facing me. If his back had been turned, I wouldn't have been able to pick him out of a lineup if the sizes were right. Might the killer have made the same mistake, even though the homicide had taken place in Star Gaze and not Star Burst?

"Is there anything else you want to know?" Hodge asked sleepily. "I never seem to get enough rest these days, but when I woke a moment ago, I heard you talking, and I couldn't just stay quiet. Go on, ask me anything."

"Does your attorney have any reason to want you dead?" I asked him.

Hodge shrugged. "I wouldn't think so."

"Is he the executor of your estate, by any chance?" Jake asked him softly.

"Yes, of course. He handles all of my personal affairs."

I saw where my husband was going. "And is there a fee he receives for handling your estate?"

Hodge looked stricken. "He gets ten percent, right off the top."

"So, he has a fairly strong financial motive to see your will probated before you set up that trust, doesn't he?" Jake asked.

"More than enough," Hodge said wearily.

"We already know how Christy Locke feels about you. She's really resentful about you buying back that stock, isn't she?"

"No matter what she says, I never took advantage of her!" Hodge protested, maybe just a little too hard. "She needed money, and I offered her a fair deal at the time to buy those shares back at the going rate. She lost faith in me, and it burned her. Can I be held accountable for that?"

"She didn't sell it all to you though, did she? Is your move going to impact her net worth?"

Hodge shrugged. "As would be expected, she'll get fair market value when we liquidate. It's not a fortune, but it should be more than enough to live on if she watches her pennies."

"But if she'd held onto her stock, she wouldn't have to do that, would she?" I asked him.

"She could pretty much live any lifestyle she chose," Hodge admitted. "Sure, she could have killed London if she thought it was me. There's no doubt in my mind."

"But there's also no proof," Jake said.

"That's why you two are here, or at least that was my original intention. I never suspected that I'd be hiring my own jailers when I brought you in."

"You're not paying us though, remember?" I asked.

"I still consider you to be in my employ," he said.

"That's debatable," Jake said.

Hodge stood, clearly more weary than he had been from our conversation. "I'm not going to stand here and argue semantics with you. I'm going back to bed. Wake me up if you solve my murder, or London's."

"You're not dead yet," I reminded him.

"Evidently not from someone close to me's lack of trying, though," he replied. "It's more than a little disconcerting knowing that so many people might want to see me dead."

After Hodge was back in his room, I gathered the folders together and put them in a pile. The man had been at least partially right. The answer to our question probably wouldn't be found there, though we had gained several insights into our fellow guests while perusing their files. Evidently, only time would tell us which one turned out to be London's killer, Hodge's attempted killer, or if they were by any chance one and the same. The more I thought about it, it really was too big a stretch for me to believe that London hadn't been killed by the same person who'd tried to shoot Hodge, unless our host was the actual murderer himself. If Hodge had killed his onetime friend, for whatever reason, Jake and I wouldn't rest until we proved it, no matter what. It was our way. Once we got our teeth into a case, there was no backing off, no giving up, until the murderer was named.

I started to nod off, and Jake patted my leg. "Suzanne, why don't you take the first shift of sleep? I need to think about a few things, so I might as well stay up."

"I'm okay," I said, rubbing my face with my hands. "I'll stay up with you."

"Nonsense. Get some rest. I'll wake you in four hours, and then you can take over for me. It's not ideal, but it should be enough rest to get us both through tomorrow."

I glanced back into Hodge's bedroom as I asked my husband softly, "Do you think he might have killed his friend, or was it really just a case of mistaken identity?"

"I wish I knew," Jake answered softly. "I just hope I never have so many people interested in seeing me dead as there are who want to see the end of him."

"Being rich comes with its own problems, doesn't it?" I asked.

"It doesn't have to. I believe it all depends on how you live your life. I'm beginning to suspect that Hodge has more to answer for than we know. I'm not very happy about him eavesdropping on his guests, whether he has consent or not."

"Me either, but none of that necessarily makes him a killer," I reminded my husband.

"I know that. It still makes me wonder what's really going on here," he said. "I feel as though we're missing something, but I can't quite put my finger on it."

"Well, I'll leave it in your most capable hands," I said as I stifled another yawn. "If you're absolutely certain, I'm going to take you up on that offer to sleep first."

"I think that's a fine idea," he said with a soft smile.

I didn't rest my head yet, though. "Let's get one thing clear, though. If I wake up in the morning and discover that you let me sleep through the night, you and I are going to have a problem, sir. Do we understand each other?"

He saluted with a smile. "Loud and clear. See you in four hours."

And with that, I nodded off, not sure what I might find when I woke up the next time.

CHAPTER 14

THE NEXT THING I REALIZED, Jake was shaking my shoulder. "Wake up, sleepyhead. It's time for your shift."

"Did anything happen while I was asleep?" I asked as I sat up from the couch and rubbed my eyes.

"No, he's been in there sleeping like a baby, and nothing has occurred out here, either."

"So tell me, did you come up with any great insights while I was asleep?" I asked him.

"No, I'm afraid I'm just as stumped as I was when you nodded off."

"Well, try to let your mind rest and get some sleep. It's going to be morning before you know it, and we have a busy day ahead of us."

"Yes, full of scavenger hunts and murder investigations. In retrospect, allowing the games to continue seems a little silly, doesn't it?"

"I'm not so sure about that," I replied. "It will give us a chance to observe our suspects without them realizing we know that London was murdered. I'm sure the killer is biting his nails wondering when the body is going to be discovered." A sudden thought struck me. "There's a very real possibility that whoever did it thinks that Hodge is dead. Maybe we should have our host hide up here tomorrow while the scavenger hunt is taking place?"

"Why would we do that?" Jake asked.

"Well, what if the killer thinks he's struck our host down? If

Hodge shows himself, it might afford the murderer another crack at him before he can sign that paperwork selling his holdings."

"And what if London's real killer is sleeping just over there?" Jake asked me softly as he pointed to Hodge.

"It still won't hurt having him hide out," I reasoned. "Besides, we can't babysit him the entire time we have left on the island. What do you think?"

"At this point, I'm not sure what we should do," Jake said as he stretched. "The truth is, I'm exhausted. I'll leave you to figure it out while I'm resting. At least it will give you something productive to think about while you're watching Hodge."

"As if there weren't enough things to consider the way everything stood before I brought that up," I said with a smile. I gave Jake a quick kiss, and before I knew it, my husband was fast asleep. I was glad that I'd taken the second shift of watching our host. After all, the hours were much more in line with my regular donut-making schedule. How I longed for the simplicity of being back in my kitchen mixing up batters and doughs instead of trying to solve a murder and perhaps prevent another one.

I found myself glancing through the files again searching for something productive to do, and then I realized that we'd ignored the staff's entries entirely. The real question there was why would any of them want to see their employer dead? Oddly enough, there were comments on every last one of them, with one exception. Cyn's entry was the last one in the file, and it was blank beyond the basic information contained in everyone else's dossiers. Hodge must have run out of time to comment on her time with him, and I was sorry that he hadn't had a chance to write anything about her. His comments on Mrs. Bellacourt alone were rather startling, and what Hodge wrote about her caught my eye.

Belle somehow found out about the substantial inheritance

she'll receive when I die, but things got complicated recently. She came to me and told me about her nephew's operation. Belle wanted an advance against her salary, but she would have had to work a hundred years to pay it all back. I turned her down, but then I secretly made arrangements to pay all of the lad's hospital bills anonymously. That might have been a mistake. Could Belle have decided to get her bequest early when I refused her request? Maybe I should tell her what I did. No, doing something like that sticks in my throat. Good deeds aren't supposed to be acknowledged. Besides, Belle wouldn't kill me, not even for her beloved Nathan.

Would she?

It all made for very interesting reading. Hodge's comments on Nan's cleaning abilities, Choonie's cooking expertise, and Harley's simplified thought processes made me wonder how much he'd really bonded with the rest of his staff. All in all, it made for light reading, but by the time I was finished leafing through the files, I was no closer to a solution than I'd been before.

By the time I roused Jake, I still hadn't been able to come up with any better plan than we already had in place. "I'm afraid I've failed you miserably as a tactician," I admitted as my husband came awake.

"Don't beat yourself up about it," Jake said as he peeked in on Hodge, who was still snoring quite loudly. "At least you accomplished your main task. Our host is still with us."

"I'm not at all sure I should get much credit for that," I said. "I still think we should leave him up here, with one change."

"What's that?"

"He has to show us his surveillance equipment first."

"So we can use it?" Jake asked.

"No, I was thinking we should disable it," I admitted.

"Maybe we shouldn't," Jake said after a moment's pause.

"Why not?"

"If Hodge is innocent, he might be able to pick up on something someone says that slips right past us. We might as well treat him as an ally for now, at least until we know any better."

I didn't like the thought of our host snooping on us, but Jake made a valid point. After all, we'd all signed those waivers, and though I loathed the violation of our privacy, if it could help us catch a killer, I was willing to bend my personal rules a little to do so.

"What's all the hubbub out here?" Hodge asked as he joined us.

"We want to see your equipment," I said.

"Pardon me?" he asked, rubbing his face with both hands.

"The surveillance equipment," Jake corrected.

"Why?" The suspicion was clear in his voice.

"We figure that while you're up here, you might as well listen in and give us your take on things from your perspective," Jake said.

"And you agreed to this?" he asked me.

"I stand by my husband," I replied.

"That's not really an answer though, is it?"

"Maybe not, but it's all that you're getting," I said, not breaking our eye contact. He needed to learn that two could play it cagy.

"Very well," Hodge said as he walked over to what had appeared to be a plain paneled wall. After placing his thumb on what I'd assumed was just another knot in the wood, part of the panel opened up before my very eyes. Hidden behind it was an array of equipment that would do any modern spy proud. All of the monitors were dark, but three dials lit up when he hit the power button, and I could suddenly hear the staff preparing for breakfast.

"Who wants to bet that there will be special orders for breakfast from this gang?" Nan said, her voice coming in clearly distinctive over the system.

"They can ask all they want, but Hodge won't allow it," Cyn said. "I don't blame him, either. It's an odd group he's gathered here, isn't it?"

"I don't know. We've had odder," Harley chimed in. Evidently he'd been drafted to help the kitchen staff while they were shorthanded, though Cyn had protested otherwise.

"What are you all talking about?" another voice asked.

"We were just discussing breakfast, Choonie," Cyn said.

"As long as you can work and talk at the same time, I don't care if you discuss global warming," the cook said.

A door opened, and a new, familiar voice spoke. "I trust you are close to being finished with your preparations? Breakfast is to be served in seven minutes." It was unmistakably Mrs. Bellacourt.

"Yes, ma'am," Choonie said, with the others chorusing in their acquiescence as well.

"Very good." After a moment's pause, she added, "I know that I don't need to remind you that gossiping about our guests is strictly against the rules."

"No, ma'am, you don't," Nan said, with Cyn and Choonie echoing the sentiment.

"Harley?" Mrs. Bellacourt asked.

"What? Yes. No. Whatever the right answer is, that's mine," he said.

"Very well. Back to work, all of you," she said as she clapped her hands together.

"Wow, I can't believe how clear everything sounds," I remarked.

"You should have seen the video feed," Hodge replied. "It's all state of the art and top of the line."

"I'm sure it's amazing," Jake said. "We'll touch base with

you a little later to find out if you've gained any insights from your listening."

"I should be down there with you," Hodge said stubbornly.

"There are a great many reasons that is a bad idea," Jake explained. "We want to keep the element of surprise in our favor. If the killer thinks their victim last night was you, they may be pushed into making a mistake. If you show yourself, we have nothing to gain by it."

"It makes sense, Hodge," I said, backing my husband.

"I still don't like it," he said. "You honestly think I killed London, don't you?"

"We're still reserving judgment," I answered. "If you were in our position, wouldn't you?"

"If I were you, I'd let me do as I please. After all, it is my island."

"And your life," Jake said. "If you choose to risk it foolishly, there's nothing we can do about it."

He clearly didn't like my husband's response at all. "What am I supposed to eat while you're both down there feasting on Choonie's food?"

"I'm sure one missed meal won't kill you," I said sweetly.

"That's easy for you to say. You'll be getting breakfast, won't you?"

Since I didn't have a comment, I didn't reply. I asked my husband, "Jake, what do we do about a fresh change of clothes?"

"All of our things are in our cottage," he said. "We can change later, but for now, we need to get downstairs and not worry about showing up in yesterday's clothing."

"Fine," I said, not happy about wearing the same thing I had on the day before but understanding that we were in a bit of a time crunch.

"There's just one thing we need to deal with before we go," Jake said.

"Are you honestly going to lock me up?" Hodge asked.

"In a way. Can you program the system so that only Suzanne and I have access to the elevator for the near future?"

"If I input your thumbprint scans, I can handle that easily," he said.

"And can you lock yourself out from using the elevator?" I asked him.

He nodded, but it was clear that he wasn't happy about the prospect. "What if there's an emergency? You don't want to leave me stuck up here, do you?"

"It's better than the alternative," I said.

"What's that?"

"Stumbling across your dead body later because you wouldn't listen to us," I said bluntly. It had been a brutal thing to say, but I needed to get through to him that if *he* hadn't killed London, he needed to realize that whoever had still wanted him dead.

"Point taken," he said. "Come on. It will only take a few seconds."

We all walked to the elevator, and after removing a panel, Hodge instructed Jake and I to place our thumbs on a touchscreen. A few moments after that, our host punched in a few codes and then closed the panel back up. "Go on. Try it."

I placed my thumb on the summoning button, and sure enough, it opened.

Jake wasn't satisfied, though. He let the door close, and then he instructed Hodge to do the same thing.

Our host shot my husband a dirty look, took off the access panel, entered a few new codes into the system, and then closed it back up. After that, no matter how many times he tried, Hodge couldn't summon the elevator to his own penthouse suite. "Satisfied?"

"For now," Jake said as he placed his thumb on the button.

The door opened promptly at his command.

"We'll see you soon," I said, and Jake and I rode down together, leaving Hodge fuming on the floor above us.

CHAPTER 15

BREAKFAST WAS A BUFFET FILLED with various scrumptious items, and I loaded my plate. For some reason I was starving, and there was no excuse not to indulge in the goodies laid out for us. The eggs were done to perfection, the bacon was of a quality and cut that I'd only dreamed about, the fruit was top notch, and the juices were clearly all freshly squeezed, despite the season. I glanced over and saw that Jake's plate was stacked high as well with all kinds of things that were bad for him, including enough bacon, ham, sausage, and steak to choke a carnivore, but I decided to let him have a free pass. After all, one meal couldn't destroy his cholesterol levels completely, could it?

"Where's our host this morning?" Barry Day asked us after we'd all settled in to our meal. Only the guests were eating, and Mrs. Bellacourt had stationed herself near the kitchen alongside Nan and Cyn. I supposed that Choonie was in back making even more goodies for us, and where Harley might be was beyond me.

"He may or may not be joining us today," Mrs. Bellacourt said. "I've been instructed to lead the day's activities."

When had Hodge given her those instructions? Was she lying, vamping while her boss was absent, or had Hodge found a way to communicate with her despite our interference? That was one of the questions I was going to ask our host the next time I saw him, but for the moment, I decided to keep what I knew to myself.

"Did someone just ask about me?" an all-too-familiar voice asked from the entrance to the dining room.

Why hadn't Jake and I known on some level that this was coming? Of course Hodge could just as easily program his own thumbprint back into the system as soon as we'd left him. I found myself staring at him instead of doing what I should have been doing, which was watching the faces of the other guests. If any of them had been startled by his sudden appearance, they'd had the chance to recover before I saw them. I hoped Jake had the foresight to watch everyone as Hodge had walked in, but evidently he'd been just as caught off guard as I had been.

As our host grabbed a plate, he said with a crooked grin, "Initially, I was going to forego today's festivities, but then I decided that I couldn't pass up such an excellent-looking meal. Choonie really knows how to throw a great breakfast, doesn't she?" He glanced over at Jake and me, and his only sign of acknowledgment that he'd broken our agreement with us was a slight shrug in our general direction. Jake was right. If the man was foolish enough to take his life into his hands by acting so recklessly, then his blood would be on his own head and not ours. We'd done everything we could to protect him, but he'd crossed a line, and there was no going back now. The only thing I wondered about was if he'd done it knowing that the killer couldn't strike at him, and that meant that he'd killed London Peale himself, despite his earlier protests to the contrary.

Carl Wilson abandoned his plate and walked hurriedly toward his employer. Was he going to strike him down in front of all of us, given the unexpected opportunity? I saw Jake tense too, but Carl only offered his hand. "Boss, I need a moment alone with you. It's urgent."

Even Hodge wasn't foolish enough to do that, given the circumstances. "Whatever you've got to say, you can say it in front of everyone here," Hodge replied, tensing up as well. Maybe our host was innocent after all. Either that, or he was doing a fine job of acting frightened by the attorney's bold approach.

I had held my breath a moment before Wilson held out his hand, but upon seeing it, I allowed it to escape.

Hodge took the man's hand reluctantly, and then just as quickly released it. "What's this all about, Wilson?"

"I'm leaving," he said.

"I'm afraid that's out of the question," Hodge said. I hoped he didn't mention the damaged boat. I wanted to hold at least a few secrets back so we could investigate the murder without showing *all* of our cards.

"I'm sorry, but it's a done deal, boss," Wilson said. He reached into his jacket pocket, and I tensed yet again, but instead of a weapon, the attorney simply pulled out an envelope.

"What's this?" Hodge asked as he received it.

"It's my resignation, effective immediately," Wilson said. "Let's face it. You don't need me anymore, sir. Let a younger man oversee the dismantling of your organization. In three days' time, I'll be in France enjoying my retirement."

"Can you afford to do that?" Hodge asked him.

"I've made some wise investments over the years, and I've saved my money, too. I'm set for life if I live conservatively, and to be honest with you, serving as your attorney is killing me with stress. Yesterday I was ready to climb over everyone else's bodies to win the prize you were dangling in front of all of us, but sometime in the middle of the night, I realized that I'd become something I promised myself I'd never be, and I didn't like it."

"What about acting as my executor? You'll at least still do that, won't you?"

"Again, I'm sorry to disappoint you, but no, I'm giving up my practice altogether," Wilson said. I could swear I saw the years fall off the man as he tendered his resignation. "I'm sure you'll find someone more than capable of handling things when the time comes."

"That's a great deal of money you're giving up. You realize that, don't you?" Hodge asked him, as though he were surprised by the attorney's actions as well as his motivation.

"Maybe so, but it's still not worth the price I'd have to pay to earn it," Wilson said. "Anyway, this is the right time for me to leave. Oh, I'll stay and participate in your little scavenger hunt today, but I have no delusions that I'm going to win. Your little contest last night made up my mind for me. Hodge, I'm tired of jumping through someone else's hoops. From now on, I bend my knee to no man."

It was a rather dramatic statement, and I wasn't sure how the others would react to it. Applause was out of the question, though it wouldn't have been out of place, at least not in my mind.

Instead, all I heard was the word "sucker" come from Barry Day's direction.

The rest of us pretended not to hear it, and Carl Wilson looked a little embarrassed as he added, "Anyway, I wanted to tell you face to face. It's done, so let's get on with breakfast, shall we?"

Hodge, still looking dumbfounded, nodded and absently finished filling up his plate.

Without realizing what he'd done, Carl Wilson had just taken his name off our list of suspects. After all, his only motivation had been winning the executor's prize, and he'd just given that up. We currently had plenty of viable suspects, though. Besides Mrs. Bellacourt, and to a lesser extent the rest of the staff, we still had Barry Day, Molly Rider, and Christy Locke on our list.

There were no more surprises at breakfast, not that we hadn't just had two rather big ones, and Hodge took center stage as the staff got busy clearing away the breakfast dishes. On his way to the front of the room, I noticed our host have a whispered conversation with Harley, who, after a moment's puzzled look, nodded and then left the lodge. What was that all about? I didn't have a chance to find out as Hodge cleared his throat, a simple act that got everyone's attention.

"Thank you all for joining me," Hodge said as he looked around the room. "As a reminder, Mr. Day won the first round last night, but today's scavenger hunt will be worth three times the points, so it's still anyone's game."

It was not only patently unfair, but the announcement had come totally out of the dark. In one fell swoop, Hodge had just negated Barry Day's win the night before. I glanced over at the young shark and noticed that his smile only broadened at the news. It was as though he'd been expecting something along those lines, but there was steel in his gaze as well, showing that he was none too pleased with it.

When Barry Day didn't react, I could swear that Hodge looked a little disappointed. What game was this man playing, goading a potential murderer like that? The rich and powerful could be very different indeed, I decided. "Today's scavenger hunt will take place outside, all around Star Burst. The cottages are off limits, and anyone found there will be instantly disqualified." It was a clever way of keeping London Peale's body from being discovered, and I had to admire the smooth way our host had done it. He continued. "Mrs. Bellacourt will be handing out a list of six items shortly. Given that there are currently six contestants, we've seen fit to hide six of each object at every location. You should be warned that taking more than one object will lead to your immediate disqualification as well."

That got a grumble from Barry Day, who had evidently planned on cheating from the very beginning. I'd have to keep an eye on him, and not just for the scavenger hunt. Then again,

I was just as carefully trying to watch Molly, Christy, and Mrs. Bellacourt, since I knew that my final four suspects had motives of their own. At least Carl Wilson was in the clear, until we learned something that made us think otherwise.

"Can we team up with other guests?" Christy asked Hodge, glancing at Carl for a brief second.

"Yes, but if you are a member of a team, your points will be issued accordingly. Two members will be allotted half the points to each, and so on."

"So, we're better off working alone," Barry said.

"Not necessarily," Hodge replied. "Remember, with the total value today being tripled, an even split between two people still outweighs last night's victory altogether." Was it my imagination, or had Hodge taken some amount of joy by pointing that out? "Are there any more questions?"

When there were none, Hodge nodded to Mrs. Bellacourt, who proceeded to hand out the lists. Jake and I grabbed ours, but we didn't join the other contestants rushing out of the building.

Instead, we approached Hodge.

Before we could say a word, our host grinned that crooked little grin of his and said, "What can I say? I changed my mind. So sue me."

"You know that it was a foolish risk to take," Jake said.

"I wasn't all that worried. Nobody was going to try anything in front of everyone else," Hodge said.

"Maybe not," I replied, "but you don't have an audience looking on now, do you?"

"I've already taken that into consideration. I'm heading back upstairs," Hodge said. "I may seem reckless to you both, but I'm not foolish."

"That remains to be seen," I said.

He decided to let that pass. "Hadn't you both better get busy? Those objects aren't going to find themselves."

"Your scavenger hunt is the last thing on our minds at the moment," I replied, and Jake nodded in agreement. "Your life is worth more to us than the prizes you're offering, as hard as that might be for you to grasp at the moment."

"I'm touched," he said. "I really am." I looked for signs that he was being sarcastic, but I didn't find any. The man was actually being sincere. Then again, I'd once heard a comedian say that once you learned how to fake sincerity, the rest of it was all downhill. "Don't worry. I'll go back to my aerie now."

"Is there any chance you'll stay there, though?" Jake asked him.

"I'm not making any promises. We'll just have to wait and see," he said.

Why was I not surprised to hear that?

Hodge walked to the elevator, and naturally enough, we walked with him. Tapping the list in my hand, he said, "You really should play. I'm certain the money would come in handy for a donutmaker and a retired cop."

"We're both more than that, and you know it," Jake said icily.

"Of course you are," Hodge said in a conciliatory fashion. "I just want you to get something out of this besides the satisfaction of saving my life, since you won't take a direct payment from me."

"Hopefully the satisfaction will be enough," I said.

After Hodge was gone, I glanced down at the list in my hand. The following six items had been printed in plain script:

A blue coin
A black circle
A golden ring
A yellow whistle
A white knight
A brass key

"What's this man's fascination with colors?" I asked Jake.

"I don't know, but this is a rather eclectic list, isn't it? Where are the clues, anyway?" my husband asked as he flipped the paper over to reveal nothing but blank space there.

"This must be strictly a hunting game," I said. "Did you notice something?"

"Do you mean other than the fact that we're searching for a murderer while the rest of our suspects are out hunting the grounds looking for six inane objects?"

"Hodge didn't say anything about anyone else grabbing a clue once someone else found it. Last night there was a waiting period, but today it's a free-for-all."

"I suppose that makes it more exciting for him," Jake said.

"And it makes it all a bit more cutthroat, too, doesn't it? How are we going to get our suspects to talk to us if they're afraid we're just trying to snatch up their clues?"

Jake thought about that for a moment, and then he said, "It's simple. We just ignore the rules."

"Generally I'm a pretty law-abiding citizen, but I'm up for anything. What did you have in mind?"

"I think we should examine the other cottages to see what we can learn about our suspects," Jake replied. "Are you okay with giving up a chance at the grand prize if we're caught?"

"I can live with it if you can," I said with a grin. "Where should we look first?"

"Since Molly is staying at the lodge, let's leave her place for last. I'll let you pick. Christy Locke or Barry Day?"

"Let's go with Christy's place first," I said.

"Sounds good to me," Jake said. "Is there any reason in particular that you want to start with her?"

"Let's just call it a hunch and leave it at that," I said.

"That sounds good to me. Suzanne, I've learned over time not to discount your hunches," he said, and despite what the rules said, we went off in search of clues that might help us find London Peale's killer.

CHAPTER 16

" **I** THINK WE MADE IT HERE without being seen," I said as we walked into Star Fire, the cottage where Christy Locke was staying. It had an identical layout to our cottage, so it was easy enough to search the place for some kind of clue. Jake went straight for her luggage, while I decided to check the less obvious places. We didn't find anything out of the ordinary until I happened to glance at the nightstand. Sitting there in plain sight was something marked "My Journal," and out of curiosity, I flipped it open to the last entry. "Jake, listen to this," I said as I read the woman's private thoughts. I felt a little uneasy doing it, but the fact that we were looking for a murderer eased my sense of guilt, at least a little bit, anyway.

"*That's it. I give up. I'm tired of holding onto past resentments. When Hodge bought back my shares, I was angry, not only with him, but with the world in general, and more importantly, with myself. These stupid little games he has us playing has shown me yet again that having money is in no way related to being happy. If I admit it to myself, I'm happier now than I've ever been in my life. So I'm letting my past resentments go to start living my life in the here and now. Who knows? Maybe he did me a favor by ridding me of too much money. I know the destructive path I'd been on would have ended me if I hadn't stopped what I'd been doing, and not having so much money allowed me to walk away from it all. I should give him a big fat kiss for relieving me of all of that pressure, but on second thought, I think I'll just smile and walk away. I've been hanging onto him for a long time, hoping that he'd feel remorse for what he'd done to me, but after I leave here this weekend, I'm vowing never to see him again. I can wish him good luck, but I don't want him in my life anymore. Today is in fact a new beginning for me, and he's welcome to everything he has. It's truly time to turn my back on my old life and begin anew."*

"Does that sound like a woman who's just committed murder to you?" I asked Jake.

"No, it doesn't," he said. "Is there any chance she wanted someone to find it, though? Let's say she killed London and then crept back in here, remorseful for her actions, and she decided to try to lay a false trail for whoever might investigate this."

"I don't buy it, and I know in my heart that neither do you," I said. "You've met Christy. I'm not saying she isn't capable of committing murder. I just don't think she'd be calm enough to try to cover it up by writing something like this in her diary to throw us off her scent."

"You're right. It's beyond belief that she could do that. Should I just stop looking?"

"No, while we're here, we should keep searching the place. Just because she didn't kill London doesn't mean she didn't take those shots at Hodge."

I glanced through the remainder of the journal, searching for any sign that she might have done anything like attempting to murder our host. Something caught my eye, but it had nothing to do with Hodge, at least not directly. "I found something else," I said.

"Read it to me," Jake urged me.

"There was another mass shooting today. What's wrong with this country? When did this become a way of dealing with an unhappy or unfulfilled life, by sowing death? It never fails to remind me that I nearly killed my little brother forty years ago with my father's rifle. I can still see the terrified look on Robbie's face as the gun

discharged. Thank goodness I missed him! I'd been a child myself, and yet I'd nearly taken my own brother's life. I understand that many folks believe that guns have their place in this world, but I hope I never see one again as long as I live."

"Wow, that must have been truly traumatic for her," I said as I closed up the diary. "Can you imagine that the woman who wrote this ever took three shots at Hodge?"

"Suzanne, it's pretty clear that we're facing a dead end here. Let's go over to Star Shine and see what we can find at Barry Day's place."

"Agreed," I said, sorry that I'd violated Christy's privacy but happy that I could take her name off our list of suspects. We were now looking at Barry Day, Molly Rider, and Mrs. Bellacourt, and at this point, I could imagine any one of them taking those shots at Hodge or driving an ax into London Peale's back in the dark.

Barry Day's cottage was a mess, which surprised me, given the general neatness of the man whenever I'd seen him. Jake started in on his briefcase, while I tackled the man's suitcase this time.

Jake called me over before I'd had much more time than to take a perfunctory look in the bag.

"He's leaving, too," Jake said as he handed me a sheaf of papers.

"What do you mean? Barry Day is much too young to retire," I said.

"I don't mean he's quitting work, I'm talking about leaving Hodge's company. Look at that." He pointed to the top page, and I read a note from Jeb Barton, CEO of Barton Industries. It welcomed Barry into the fold and had his starting date listed as the next week. Evidently Barry had failed in his takeover attempt and had quickly moved to secure his own future without Hodge Castor being a part of it.

"Do you think Hodge knows about this?" I asked Jake.

"I doubt it. Does our host seem like a kind and forgiving man to you?"

"Those aren't two words I'd use to describe him," I said. "I'm not saying he's a bad guy, but he's driven, and he loves to win at everything he does. Losing Barry Day, even if he doesn't want his services anymore, isn't something Hodge would take graciously."

"This kind of kills Barry's motivation to kill for the company, don't you think?" Jake asked as he took the cover letter, folded it, and slipped it into his pocket.

"Should we honestly take that? Won't Barry know what we did?"

"I don't want to take the chance that he comes back in here and destroys the evidence later," Jake said. "It would be counterproductive for him to discard his own alibi, but he might not be thinking along those lines. Hodge needs to see this."

"Okay, if you think so," I said. "Should we have taken the diary as well?" It was bad enough reading Christy Locke's personal thoughts and feelings, but taking them pushed things to an entirely different level that I wasn't at all comfortable with.

"No, there's no need. We know her feelings, and that's all that counts. Besides, *she's* not hiding anything from Hodge."

"Okay. Are we still thinking that our host is guilty of murder, or have you changed your mind about the possibility that Hodge killed London himself?"

"You know what? I don't think so anymore," Jake said after a moment's pause.

"What brought about your change of heart?"

"I've been thinking about his actions since we found the body," Jake explained. "If he'd killed London, I don't think he would have shown his face at breakfast this morning."

"Why not? If he didn't do it, wouldn't he be afraid that he'd be next?" I asked, playing devil's advocate. "He had more reason to hide than he did to expose himself like that."

"That's the trap I was in before as well, but Hodge doesn't process things like we do. When he's challenged in any way, his habit is to confront his antagonist, not hide away. You saw how he openly challenged Barry Day this morning, and you heard his reaction to Carl Wilson's resignation. I don't see him as a cowering kind of guy, unless he was trying to convince us of his innocence by acting afraid. Does that line of reasoning make any sense to you?"

"From Hodge, it makes perfect sense, though I'd have trouble convincing anyone else that was what happened. I know what you mean, though. Hodge is a great many things, but stupid doesn't even crack the list."

Jake continued his line of thought. "Let's say he did kill London Peale, for whatever reason. Would he just stand there holding the murder weapon, waiting for someone to discover him, if he had? The man prides himself on his split-second decisions. Unless we literally stumbled upon him a few seconds after the murder, I'm inclined to think that he might not have done it."

I still wasn't sure, but my husband had dealt with a great many more killers than I had, thank goodness for that. The hiding part I agreed with, at any rate. Hodge would try to face a charging bull down; there was no way I could see the man just turning tail and running. "Okay, for argument's sake, let's say that Hodge is everything he's claimed to be, a potential murder victim who brought us here to solve the case. That means that our theory that London's murder was a case of mistaken identity is still a sound one. Given the lack of motive on Carl Wilson's part, not to mention Barry Day and Christy Locke, that leaves just two suspects on our list."

"If you hadn't read Hodge's description of what happened with Mrs. Bellacourt, I would have never even considered her. As a matter of fact, I still think Molly Rider might be the killer."

"But we can't take Hodge's assistant off our list, either," I said. "Ordinarily I'd suspect that she's no killer, but if she believed she was doing it for a good cause, and that her employer was going to be dead within the year anyway, I wouldn't have a bit of trouble with believing it. There's ice in that woman that scares me more than a little bit, and I'm not afraid to admit it."

"If you look at it that way, it makes perfect sense, at least from her perspective," Jake said. "Let's go back to the lodge and see if we can sneak into Molly Rider's room. I'd like to have more than a hunch to go on before I start accusing her of murder."

"Agreed," I said, and we left Star Shine and headed back to Star Burst, the main lodge.

We were getting closer, that much was certain. I could feel it in my bones.

I only hoped we managed to unmask the killer before she finally succeeded in what she seemed to be so intent on doing, which was killing Hodge Castor.

We didn't make it back to the lodge, though, at least not right away.

There was an argument going on when we approached the main building, and before we knew what was happening, we were being dragged into it, whether we wanted to be or not.

"You took more than one key!" Barry Day shouted at Christy Locke as we approached. "I saw you!"

"I did not!" Christy protested as she held a small brass skeleton key aloft. "See? I have just the one I took!"

"Then why are three missing?" Barry asked loudly as he looked into the nearly buried container that had housed the set of golden keys mentioned on the list.

"It's easy, if you use your head for something other than keeping your ears apart. Someone must have gotten here before me," she protested.

"Why are you so intent on winning, anyway? I thought you'd given up money and all that garbage about finding a better life. That's what you told me an hour ago, anyway. What happened, did you change your mind yet again?"

"I'm not after the money," she told him coldly.

"Well, I'm sure you don't want any more of Hodge's time than you've already had," Day said derisively. It was clear that he'd been stung by Hodge's earlier words, and he was overjoyed finding someone to take his ire out on.

"You're right about that, at any rate. I wouldn't take that hour if it came wrapped in a bow."

"What is it then, the land? What's so great about a piece of property?"

"You're only saying that because you have no soul," Christy said, trying to keep her temper in check. "I've walked that land a hundred times, and let me tell you, it's one of the most tranquil places I've ever been to in my life. If I were to own that, I could build a modest retreat and get away from all of the materialistic greed that seems to consume us all."

"Oh, and you're so much better than the rest of us, fully evolved and all of that, are you?" he asked her.

"No, but I never claimed to be. Only that I'm trying."

"I don't care. You can have your little getaway, but you won't get it by cheating."

At that moment, Cyn appeared, looking quite sternly at the arguing adults.

"What's going on here?" she asked.

Before any of us could say a word, Barry Day shouted, "She's cheating," as he pointed to Christy Locke.

"I am not," Christy said, keeping her voice calm and level despite the accusation. "Ask them. They saw everything," she added as she pointed to us.

"I'm afraid we came to this late," I said. "We only just got here when Barry started shouting."

"And where exactly were the two of you?" he asked us, glaring at both of us simultaneously. "Looking out of bounds, were you?"

"Why would we risk that?" I asked, trying to couch my response in a way that would resonate with this young, lean, and hungry man. "We want the prize, too."

"The land as well, no doubt?" he asked us, the sneer obvious.

"For all I care, you can have the time and Christy can have the land, but we're interested in the money," I said.

That earned me looks of disapproval from both Jake and Cyn, but I didn't care. I didn't want to let on that Jake and I had been snooping, at least not until it was time to reveal what we'd uncovered. If the others thought a little less of me in the meantime, then so be it.

"That doesn't change the fact that she took two keys," Barry said.

"May I see your collection of objects?" Cyn asked her.

"What good would that do? She could have taken one and hidden the other," Barry protested.

"Strip search me if you want," Christy said, holding her arms out. "I don't mind one bit."

"There's no need for that," Cyn said as she took out a wand of some sort.

"What's that?"

"It will show if she's hiding any metal on her person," she explained.

"But brass won't necessarily show up in a scan, and neither will most of the other items on this list," Barry protested.

Cyn grinned. "Not ordinarily, but Hodge prepared for this possibility. Why would you expect anything less from him? Each item contains enough metal to show up with this detector. If she's hiding anything, I'll know it." The wand sweep was clean, proving that Christy hadn't absconded with too many clues.

"That still doesn't mean that she didn't just throw it away," he said sullenly.

Cyn looked at the stash of keys and said, "That's not possible, either. Each item has been accounted for. No key is missing."

"This is all garbage," Barry Day said as he stomped up the pathway back toward the lodge.

"Thanks for that," Christy said to Cyn.

"I'm just following orders," the young woman said with a grin as she swept a bit of her lustrous hair behind her ear, a gesture I hadn't seen before.

"Aren't you two going to grab your keys while you're here?" Cyn asked us with that familiar crooked grin.

"What? Oh, yes. Of course," I said. I took a key, and Jake got one for himself.

"Keep looking. I'm sure you'll turn up more clues soon," Cyn said as she headed back up the path toward the lodge.

"Jake, I just figured it out," I said once the young woman was gone.

"You know who the killer is?" he asked incredulously.

"No, but it's nearly as important as that. I need to talk to Hodge, and I mean right now."

CHAPTER 17

"You're kidding," Jake said as he listened to my theory as we headed into the lodge. "It's awfully circumstantial, isn't it?"

"Maybe, but if I'm right, Hodge already knows. Let's go find out what's really going on."

"Remember, we're still looking for a killer," Jake reminded me. "Either Mrs. Bellacourt or Molly Rider is most likely a murderer."

"I know that, but what if we aren't the only ones who know about Cyn's situation? If one of them realizes who she is, she could be in real danger. One way or the other, we need to find out."

"But we just saw her!" Jake protested. "She was fine."

"I shouldn't have to tell you of all people how quickly things can change," I said.

"You're right. Come on. I just hope our host is still upstairs, tucked safely away in his penthouse where no one else can get to him. What are the odds he did as we asked?"

"I'd say it's a coin flip at this point," I admitted as I pressed my thumb to the panel.

To my relief, the elevator door came to my summons, but it didn't open up right away. Maybe Hodge had done what we'd asked him to do after all, but I wouldn't believe it until I saw him in the penthouse with my own two eyes.

Our host looked up guiltily as the elevator door opened. "What are you two doing up here?"

"We need to talk," I said sternly.

"About the killer?"

"No, about your daughter, Cyn," I said.

Hodge's white face was enough to tell me that I'd scored a direct hit, though he tried his best to cover it up. "What are you talking about?"

"You might as well drop the pretense," Jake told him. "Suzanne figured it out."

"How?" was all that he could ask, clearly a defeated man.

"The crooked grin was the first clue. Yours both match, did you know that? Then there are the strawberry birthmarks you both share. I would have twigged to it sooner, but I just saw Cyn's behind her ear. She wears her hair down all of the time, so I can be forgiven for not noticing that earlier."

"Lots of people have strawberry birthmarks," Hodge protested feebly.

"Not that many. Besides, you told us yourself that you loved someone twenty years ago, and that's somewhere around Cyn's age, unless I miss my guess. Add her mother's bedtime stories about her father being rich and powerful, and it suddenly becomes too many coincidences to ignore."

"Her mother actually told her about me? But she doesn't *know* that I'm her father," Hodge said strongly.

"I don't think she realizes it's you, if that gives you any comfort. What we want to know is why haven't you told her?"

"It's complicated," Hodge said weakly.

"If I had a daughter out there somewhere, she'd know it, and there wouldn't be anything in the world that would stop me from telling her," Jake said. He'd lost a wife and an unborn child in the same accident, so I knew that he was speaking from the heart. It was a pain that he'd never get over; all he could manage was to subdue it, but never for very long.

"I know you're right," Hodge said, for once sounding not at all rich or powerful, either. "I've tried a dozen times, but I can't seem to bring myself to do it. Her mother didn't want me to tell her after Cyn was born, and like a fool, I respected her wishes. I didn't want to complicate my life, probably, or some selfish reason like that. When I found out Ramona had died suddenly, I had my people reach out to Cyn and offer her a job here on the island immediately."

"Where you could keep an eye on her?" Jake asked harshly.

"No, I wanted a place where I could get to know her. I've been spending a great deal of time getting acquainted with my daughter since she's been here. I'm proud of her, and I've grown to love her as a person as well."

"Don't tell us," I said. "Tell her."

"Don't you think I want to?" he asked, tears coming to his eyes.

It was time to be blunt with the man yet again. "Hodge, she's lost her mother, and her father is going to die within a year from natural causes if a killer doesn't take care of him first. What are you waiting for? Hasn't she been through enough? She deserves to know. You owe at least that much to her."

My words slapped the man worse than any hand could do, and Jake looked at me warily. I knew I'd pushed Hodge, perhaps too far, but he needed a wakeup call, and I was just the woman to give it. "I'm waiting for an answer."

"Suzanne," Jake said softly, his inflection begging me to back off, but that was one thing I knew that I couldn't do. Hodge had to take action, and he had to do it before it was too late.

"I'll go with you," I offered him, softening my voice. "Will that help?"

"Yes. Please. Both of you."

Jake smiled gently at me and nodded. Apparently I'd pushed our host just enough. "Of course, but there's another reason to hurry."

"Why is that?" Hodge asked him.

"If Suzanne could figure it out, someone else on the island could, too. If you die suddenly and Cyn can prove that she's your biological daughter, that could destroy the killer's plans. I'm not saying that Mrs. Bellacourt or Molly wouldn't have a claim against your estate, but it would certainly be muddied. The easiest way to make sure that doesn't happen would be to get rid of Cyn before anyone else finds out who she really is."

That got Hodge's attention. "Then we've got to find her!"

He hurried toward the elevator, with Jake and me close on his heels. As the lift made its way downward, Hodge asked, "Do you have any idea where she is?"

"We saw her ten minutes ago just outside the lodge," Jake said. "She can't have gone far."

"Nothing can happen to my daughter," Hodge said.

"We understand," I said.

The only problem was that the island was too large to search if we all stuck together.

Once we were outside, Jake asked me, "Any ideas?"

"I don't like it, but we're going to have to split up," I told him.

"You're not going anywhere alone," he replied. There was no doubt or hesitation in his voice as he said it.

"If Hodge goes with me, that means that you're going to be by yourself."

"I can handle myself." My husband looked around. "Where's Harley when you need him?"

"I'm afraid that's my fault," Hodge said. "I sent him out on a fool's errand. I just hope I didn't kill him in the process."

"Talk, and make it fast," Jake said.

"I don't know if you've heard, but he's been training for some kind of iron man event where he has to do a polar bear swim. He's been practicing in the lake with his wetsuit and other gear, and this morning I asked him if he could swim to shore and bring back help." Hodge glanced at his watch as he added, "He should have been back by now, though. I'm afraid he didn't make it."

There was no time to mourn the handyman, though I felt a sudden burst of sadness for another victim, however indirect, to this killer. "We'll just have to make do with what we've got, then," Jake said. He kissed me quickly, and then he took off toward the north part of the island.

"Let's go to the dock," I said. "Maybe we'll be able to see what's going on from there."

"What am I thinking?" Hodge asked. "We need to go back inside!"

"Did you forget something? Unless it's a weapon, it's going to have to wait!" I shouted as I tugged on his arm.

"You don't understand! We have the best view of the island up there," he said as he pulled me into the summoned elevator.

He was right! In our hurry to find Cyn, we'd ignored one of the major advantages we had in a search. From his aerie, we could see most of Star Island.

Hodge and I both scanned the windows, searching for some sign of the man's missing daughter, until finally I thought I spotted something near the cottage where we'd found London Peale. "Over there. What's that?" I asked.

"It looks like Cyn, but I can't see who's with her," he said, his voice nearly a wail of despair.

"Does it matter? Let's go!" I shouted.

We left the elevator, and as we burst outside, Barry Day was shouting, "I won! I won!"

Hodge and I completely ignored him.

As we ran down the path together, I found myself hoping and wishing that Cyn was okay and that the killer hadn't discovered who she really was. I didn't know if it was the adrenaline rushing through my veins or perhaps some kind of intense form of focus in my mind, but I suddenly knew who the killer had to be and why she was stalking Hodge's daughter.

It had to be Molly Rider.

She was the only one with a direct reason to wipe out any competition when it came to Hodge's estate. Mrs. Bellacourt, even if she'd been so moved to act against her employer, would receive her money no matter who the rightful heir turned out to be.

No, Molly had to be the one we'd all been searching for, and there was no doubt in my mind that she had Cyn in her clutches now.

And it was up to us to stop the killer before she could strike again.

CHAPTER 18

AT LEAST WE WEREN'T TOO late.

I took little satisfaction from the fact that Molly Rider was holding a rifle and pointing it at Cyn's head. But she hadn't pulled the trigger yet, so as far as I was concerned, we still had a slight chance to make everything right.

"Molly! Stop!" I screamed as I ran into the clearing alone. Hodge must have tripped on a tree root behind me, but I kept forging ahead until I was in the clearing. Maybe, if he used a little common sense, he'd sneak around and try to disarm Molly while I distracted her. At the very least, he could go back to the lodge for help, but either way, I didn't have time to worry about him.

"What are you doing here?" Molly shouted at me, momentarily taking her gaze off Cyn. "This is out of bounds! You're disqualified!"

Was she serious, or just seriously deranged? The woman was still talking about the scavenger hunt! "I don't care. You can have it all. It doesn't matter to me. Just don't hurt Cyn."

"What's happening, Suzanne?" Cyn cried, cowering under the rifle's point. "She wants to kill me. I don't understand!" Turning to Molly, she asked, "What did I ever do to you?"

"You were born, you silly child," Molly said. "That was all that it took."

"What does that even mean?" Cyn asked, her tears falling fast and true.

"It means that you're my daughter, and the rightful heiress," Hodge said as he stepped out from the bushes.

So, he hadn't chosen any of the options I'd hoped he'd pick.

Instead he'd done a brave but stupid thing trying to protect his only child.

"That's not funny, Hodge," Cyn said. "Why would you even say something like that?"

"Because it's true, Cynthia," he said, calling her by her full name for the first time. "Ramona was stubborn and prideful, and so was I. I asked for permission to tell you years ago, but she forbade it, and I was weak and selfish. Can you ever find it in your heart to forgive me?"

"You knew that I was your daughter all along, and you didn't tell me?" Cyn asked, her incredulity focused on her father at the moment.

"I'm ashamed to admit that's exactly what I did," he said.

"Enough of the family reunion," Molly said dismissively. "In a few minutes, none of it's going to matter, anyway."

"Do you honestly think that you can shoot all three of us before we stop you?" I asked her.

"I don't think you have the courage to try," Molly said. "I missed Hodge before, but I've been practicing since then. I won't miss again."

"How did you get a rifle onto my island?" Hodge demanded.

"I didn't *bring* a rifle," Molly said smugly, bragging. "I brought a custom fishing pole that no one bothered to check, including your precious little girl."

"I'm so sorry, Hodge," Cyn said, weeping again.

"Call me Dad, at least once," Hodge said. "Let me have that much."

"Dad," Cyn said, the word falling from her lips.

"Why did you kill London?" I asked Molly. Had Jake realized that he was chasing a dead end going after Mrs. Bellacourt? I was counting on him to play this smartly, and that meant creeping up on Molly from the side just like I'd hoped Hodge would do. If I could stall the crazed woman long enough, we all still might have a chance.

"I thought it was Hodge," Molly said, as though the admission of her mistake bothered her more than the actual murder she'd committed. "So, you knew about that, did you?"

"We've known since just after it happened. What did you use to club Harley with before you stole his ax?"

"You're more than just a donutmaker, aren't you?" she asked me. "I can see that I underestimated you from the very start. Maybe I should take care of you first."

As she swung the rifle around to point it at my torso, I saw a blur flash through the woods.

Jake had hurled his piece of firewood at her, but it hadn't struck home in time to stop her from firing off one round.

I suspected that Cyn had been hit, and when I looked over at her, I saw that she had collapsed onto the ground.

But she wasn't hit; she was holding her father's head in her lap.

Apparently, Hodge had at last done one fatherly thing in his life, perhaps the last thing he ever did.

He'd thrown himself in front of the bullet that had been meant for his daughter.

CHAPTER 19

"**D**AD? DADDY? ARE YOU OKAY?"

I gently pushed Cyn aside and saw at once that her father had been lucky. Six inches to the left, and the bullet would have pierced his heart.

As it was, he'd taken a hit in the arm.

I was sure that it was painful, but he'd literally almost dodged a bullet.

At least it hadn't been fatal.

"Put pressure on the wound with this," I said as I took a bandana from my pocket and handed it to Cyn.

She took it gratefully and pressed it against his wound, all the while crying, whether it was because she'd found her father at long last or because he'd done his best to protect her in the end when it had counted.

When I looked back at the killer, I saw that Jake had Molly's arms secured behind her, and he'd added a knee to her back to make sure she wasn't going anywhere.

"How is he?" Jake asked softly.

"He was shot in the arm, but I think he'll be okay."

"There's never a dull moment around you, is there, Suzanne?" my husband asked me with a grin.

"What can I say? I don't ask for trouble," I replied. "It just seems to find me. I'm glad you were there."

"That makes two of us," he said as we heard a boat approach

from the water, its siren wailing. "It looks like reinforcements have arrived just in the nick of time."

"Or maybe even a tad late, if you ask me," I said, touching my husband's shoulder lightly. "Thank you for saving me."

"You're most welcome," he said with a smile.

"Would you *please* get your knee out of my back?" Molly asked angrily. "You're hurting me."

"I could shoot you, if you'd rather I did that instead," Jake said. "Either way, you're not going anywhere."

Not surprisingly, that was her last request for relief.

Once Molly Rider was carted off and Hodge was being seen to by a paramedic, the rest of the group joined us.

"They wouldn't let us come down earlier," Mrs. Bellacourt said as she headed straight for her employer.

"I nearly had to tase that one," an officer agreed.

"I'm not sure it would have done any good," Hodge said with that crooked grin he shared with his daughter. "Belle, I'd like you to meet my daughter."

"What? I've known Cyn for ... Wait! Did you say daughter?"

"Yes. Isn't it wonderful?"

It took Hodge's assistant a moment to adjust to the news, but only a moment. "I think it's fabulous," she said, and then Mrs. Bellacourt surprised us all by hugging Cyn fiercely. "I'm so happy for you both that you found each other."

"Thank you," Cyn said, clearly a bit confused by her boss's show of affection.

"I still win the prize," Barry Day said, waving the found objects in the air as though they were talismans of his future fortunes. "No one had better forget that."

"If I were you, I'd choose the money, Barry," Hodge said. "After all, I'm not about to give my chief competitor any advice that he might be able to use against me. I hope you're happy at Barton. If you think I'm a tough boss, wait until you get a load of him. He makes me look like a teddy bear."

"You knew about that?" Barry Day asked, for once in his life nearly at a loss for words.

"How could you possibly think that I wouldn't?" Hodge asked him with a grin. So, that part of our spying had been unnecessary. So be it. At least the truth was coming out, one way or the other.

Looking defeated but still holding onto his last shred of dignity, Barry asked, "What does it matter, anyway? You're giving up the company, remember?"

"That was my plan before, but now I need to discuss things with my new partner."

"You have a new partner?" Barry asked him incredulously.

"Yes. I've decided that I'm keeping the business in the family. Whatever Cynthia wants to do is fine by me."

"If you don't mind, could you still call me Cyn?" she asked him haltingly.

"Your wish is my command, Cyn," he said, gripping her shoulder with his good hand.

"This has all been very exciting, but I'm afraid I must be moving on," Christy said. "I wish you all the best."

"One second," Hodge said and then asked Mrs. Bellacourt, "Do you have it with you as I asked this morning?"

"It's right here."

"Go on. Give it to her."

Mrs. Bellacourt handed Christy an official-looking piece of paper, and after taking a moment to read it, Christy Locke's eyes teared up. "It's the deed to my dream property," she said.

"Hey, what if I'd wanted that?" Barry protested. "I'm the one who won the contest."

"We both know better than that. Christy, we'll build you a

retreat on it as well. It's the least I can do. After all, you believed in me when no one else did."

She tried to hug her former partner, but it was difficult between the daughter on one side and the paramedic applying pressure to the other side. "Hodge, I don't know what to say."

"There's no need to say anything," he answered.

"We both know better than that. Thank you, my dear sweet man."

"You're very welcome," he said, before turning to Mrs. Bellacourt. "Before they haul me away, you should know something as well. Your nephew's procedure is taking place tomorrow morning. I've covered the hospital bills, as well as the recovery. If you hurry, you can make it in time before the procedure begins."

"What? But you refused my request for an advance!"

"So I did. Can't I make it a gift instead?" He looked wearily around at the group of guests. "You all should go now. You all have places you need to be and plans to make for your futures."

Jake and I had started to go as well when Hodge asked us to stay behind.

"Cyn, do you mind giving us a minute?"

"Sure. Of course," she said. "Just don't be long. We have some catching up to do."

Hodge's laughter was loud and long, and I doubted that he was feeling any pain, even from the gunshot.

Once we were alone, Hodge said, "I can't let things go like this between us."

"Listen, I'm sorry I was rough on you," I said, "but I needed to slap you hard enough to get your attention back there."

"Oh, you managed that all right, but that's not what I'm talking about. Are you certain you won't take anything from me?"

"We're sure," I said, and Jake echoed my sentiments. "What we did for you, we did out of friendship for George."

"Then know this. You two are now in possession of one of the most valuable items that exist in my world. You're getting a golden ticket, to be redeemed in any way at any time of your choosing. I will move heaven and earth to make your wish so, with no reservations. All you have to do is ask."

I didn't know how to respond, so I did what Momma had taught me to say long ago when receiving a gift. "Thank you."

"You're most welcome." He glanced over at Cyn, who was still standing in the clearing watching us, when he said, "She's really something, isn't she?"

"She really is," I said.

Hodge had learned a valuable lesson, almost too late, that when it came right down to it, family meant more than anything else.

It had almost cost him his daughter and nearly his own life learning that.

He might have been rich as far as the world was concerned, but in my opinion, my wealth greatly exceeded his.

Not only did I have everything I needed, but I had people around me who loved and cared for me, no matter what.

And that was more valuable than any golden ticket the world had to offer.

RECIPES

Gingerbread Donut Nuggets

No matter what time of year it is, we love the taste and smell of gingerbread in my house! There's something about the rich flavor that always brings smiles to our faces, and I've found myself making these treats in the middle of July just for the taste of something that reminds me of cooler temperatures and holiday decorations.

Ingredients

- 1 egg, beaten
- 1/2 cup dark-brown sugar, firmly packed
- 1/2 cup molasses
- 2 1/2 teaspoons ginger
- 2 teaspoons baking powder
- 1 teaspoon baking soda
- 1/2 teaspoon salt
- 1/2 cup sour cream
- 3 cups flour unbleached all-purpose (approximately)

Directions

Heat enough oil to fry your donut nuggets to 375 degrees F.

While the oil is coming to temperature, start by beating the egg and then adding the brown sugar and mixing it in thoroughly. Next, stir in everything except the flour, and then add just enough flour to make a soft dough, but don't overwork it.

Pull off pieces of dough the size of your thumb, round them between your palms, and then drop them into the hot oil. Keep turning the nuggets until they're dark brown all around. After you remove them from the hot oil with a slotted spoon, dust the tops with granulated sugar or dip them in melted chocolate. Either way, they make a really delightful treat!

Makes approximately 12 nuggets

Orange And Spice And Everything Nice Donuts

I'm a huge fan of orange spice anything. My late mother-in-law, a sainted woman if ever there was one, made muffins using parts of this basic recipe, but of course I had to modify it for donuts. Still, the fundamental flavors are all there, and this recipe has the added bonus of filling your kitchen with loads of wonderful aromas.

Ingredients

- 1 cup granulated sugar
- 1 cup milk (2% or whole will do nicely)
- 2 egg yolks only, beaten
- 1/2 stick butter (1/4 cup) melted
- 2 tablespoons orange extract
- 1/1/2 tablespoons canola oil
- 1 1/2 teaspoons cinnamon
- The zest of one orange, finely grated
- Candy orange slice wedges, cut into small pieces
- 3–4 cups flour
- 1 tablespoon baking powder

Directions

Mix the sugar, milk, egg yolks, melted butter, orange extract, canola oil, cinnamon, orange zest, and, if preferred, cut candy orange slice wedges until combined well. Sift the flour and baking powder together in a different bowl, then add the dry ingredients to the wet, stirring well as you go. This will make a stiff dough.

Chill the dough for at least one hour, then turn it onto a floured surface. Knead it into a ball, and then roll the ball out to ½ to ¼ inches thick. This may look a little lumpy, depending on if you used the candy wedges. Cut out the rounds.

Heat enough canola oil to fry the donuts at 375 degrees F, and then add the donut rounds and cook for 2 minutes on each side, being sure not to crowd the donuts in the pot as they cook. Drain them on a cooling rack, and then dust them with powdered sugar or eat them plain.

Makes approximately 1 dozen donuts

Easy Peasy Homemade Fried Cherry Pies

My family loves these little pies, and as an added bonus, they are a cinch to make! You can experiment with lots of different fillings (I normally stick with cherry pie or apple pie filling myself, but sometimes I feel crazy adventurous and try others as well). The truth is that most of the time, I don't bother making the fillings myself, or the crust. If you've never looked at the row upon row of pie filling available in nearly every grocery store, you're missing a sweet treat!

Give them a try! They really are delightful.

Ingredients

- Cherry pie filling, 8 oz., from the can
- 2 teaspoons sugar
- 1 teaspoon cinnamon
- 1 pie crust (ready made is fine for this recipe)

Directions

Heat the oil to 375 degrees F in a large enough container on your stovetop.

While you're waiting for it to heat up, you'll have plenty of time to prepare these jewels. Sometimes I use the filling straight from the can, and others I warm it over low heat on the stovetop before adding it to the pie crust. If you want to warm it, do so, adding the sugar and cinnamon (if preferred, though the fillings are fine without any additions).

Unroll the store-bought dough and cut circles out of it by using a donut cutter or the floured rim of a drinking glass. I like to make four fried pies from one crust, but it depends on the size of your cutter.

After the circles are cut, place a small amount of filling on one side of the dough circle (a little less than a tablespoon is usually plenty). Using your wetted finger, go around the edges of the dough and fold it in half, sealing the edges by pinching them. It will look like a half circle at this point.

Drop them into the hot oil and fry for 3 to 5 minutes, turning them halfway with a skewer so they brown equally on each side.

Once they're finished cooking, pull them from the oil with a slotted spoon and place them on a cooling rack, sprinkling them with powdered or crystallized sugar while they're still warm.

You can serve them at this point once they are cool enough, or save them for later. Either way, they make an excellent treat!

Makes 4 small pies per crust used

Ghost Cat 2: Bid for Midnight

The Cast Iron Cooking Mysteries
Cast Iron Will
Cast Iron Conviction
Cast Iron Alibi
Cast Iron Motive
Cast Iron Suspicion

46262631R00092

Made in the USA
San Bernardino, CA
01 March 2017